She felt the

Why had she bee[...]
there? And...wh[...]

'Do you mind s[...]
she asked the rug[...]
rescued her. It was late, and he was speeding [...]
one of Washington's rougher neighbourhoods.

The man seemed to give her question serious
consideration. 'Can't do that.'

'What is it with you?' she asked, agitation making
her sarcastic. 'Are you a rent-a-knight-in-shining-
armour? Have you appointed yourself my personal
guardian angel?' She laced her clammy fingers into a
knot to keep them from trembling.

A cynical grin curved the man's mouth—a mouth she
was certain rarely smiled.

'I guarantee,' he said softly in a voice that made her
shiver, '*neither* of those terms applies to *me*, but right
now you're in the safest place, under the
circumstances.'

Dear Reader,

There are some really gorgeous men in store for you in this month's Special Editions™. There's rugged Ryder Sloan, who reappears on Sara Monahan's doorstep in *Marriage Minded* written by Kayla Daniels. Predictably, he's got one thing on his mind—*marriage*! And there's also Ann Howard White's dark and dangerous Jake McAlister from *Making Memories*. He's irresistible!

We have a tantalizing new novel from the ever popular Helen R. Myers and hope you'll enjoy seeing lovers reunited in *After That Night...* Those of you who love a book with a baby and some heart-warming humour need not feel forgotten; watch how Carter MacKenzie loses control over his life, thanks to an adorable infant, in Anne McAllister's *MacKenzie's Baby*.

STRUMMEL INVESTIGATIONS by Victoria Pade finishes this month when virile Logan Strummel is baffled by *The Case of the Accidental Heiress*. And completing our six books is *Honeymoon Hotline* from Christine Rimmer—May's THAT SPECIAL WOMAN! title—where Nevada Jones tries to avoid a traditional 'alpha' male, who always gets what he wants!

Have fun!

The Editors

Making Memories

ANN HOWARD WHITE

SILHOUETTE

SPECIAL EDITION ®

*Silhouette, Silhouette Special Edition and Colophon are
registered trademarks of Harlequin Books S.A., used under licence.*

*First published in Great Britain 1997
Silhouette Books, Eton House, 18-24 Paradise Road,
Richmond, Surrey TW9 1SR*

© Ann Howard White 1996

ISBN 0 373 24067 8

23-9705

*Printed and bound in Great Britain
by Mackays of Chatham PLC, Chatham*

To Cheetah,
companion, 'writing buddy' and friend.
You were more human than feline.
We will miss you in a thousand ways.

ANN HOWARD WHITE

discovered romance straight out of three long, tedious years
of law school—and instantly fell in love. She quickly
became fast friends with a local bookseller who introduced
her to the best the genre has to offer. Sandwiched between
working with her physician/lawyer husband and raising two
daughters and a son, Ann read everything she could get her
hands on.

She completed and sold her first book and now writes full-
time. The only downside, says Ann, is how much it cuts into
her reading time.

Another novel by Ann Howard White

Silhouette Special Edition®

The Mother of His Child

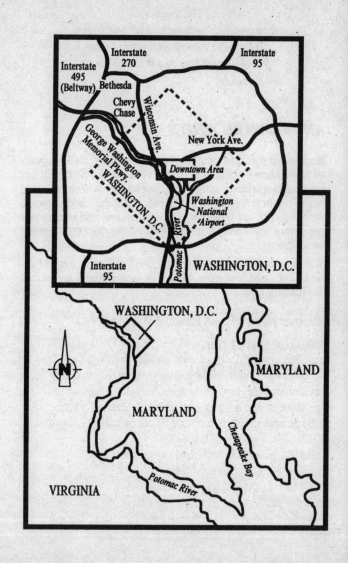

Chapter One

*W*here *in hell had the woman come from?*

Jake McAlister quickly scanned the darkened depths of the alley a few feet to his right, then jerked his gaze back to the scantily-clad figure. She was crouched behind some wooden crates stacked precariously against a wall just inside the entrance to the dead-end passageway. Damn! He'd personally checked out the area only minutes before this meeting. Except for a stray cat, several cans of vintage garbage and an assortment of boxes in various stages of dilapidation, it had been clean.

But his eyes and instincts weren't deceiving him. Somehow she'd gotten past him.

"Am I boring you, Mr. McAlister?" asked the conservatively dressed man Jake had spent the better part of six months coaxing out into the open. George Brady's voice contained the cultured tones of an Ivy

League education and grated on Jake's already edgy nerves.

"Just thinking over your offer, Brady." From his position, Jake had an unobstructed view of the intruder. Only a few feet blocked her from Brady's line of vision. Jake shifted his six-foot-three frame in an effort to distract the shorter man's attention away from the crates.

"You seem to be taking an inordinate amount of time." Brady brushed at a speck of lint on his jacket sleeve and straightened a cuff. "Do you find something more interesting than our discussion?"

Jake's mouth stretched into the semblance of a smile. "Nothing interests me more than this deal," he assured him as he took a step forward. Brady and his two companions took a step back—farther away from the woman huddled barely out of harm's way.

Adrenaline pumped through Jake's system as a frisson of panic squeezed his gut. Something told him he was about to lose control of the situation. In his line of work that was a grave error. He knew only too well that if he blew this, someone could die.

And this time it could very well be the woman hiding behind the crates.

He silently swore again. Too much was invested in this case to have it go sour because some civilian happened to stumble into the wrong place at the wrong time. Who the hell was she, anyway?

Just a little luck, that's all he'd needed. Just enough time to work a deal that would ultimately bring down Brady and the vultures that worked for him.

But then Jake couldn't remember the last time luck had been around when he'd needed it. With a loud crash, the upper crate tumbled to the ground.

Acting instinctively, Jake dived straight for the woman, now exposed to three additional pairs of eyes. As his body connected with hers, he heard her startled cry and the whoosh of breath leaving her lungs. He was aware of delicate bones, well-toned muscles and softer flesh crumpling beneath him as they hit the pavement with a jarring thud and his weight settled over her. She struggled briefly, then went still.

"Someone you know, McAlister?" Brady commented, as the dust settled. His tone conveyed displeasure and disapproval and just a hint of distress. "I didn't realize you worked with a partner."

"I don't." Jake steadied his breathing while searching furiously for an explanation to defuse a situation that had become precarious. He opted for the truth. "She must have wandered in by accident."

"Not very efficient, McAlister. You assured me this place was safe."

Jake shifted off the woman and put his body between her and the others. "You of all people should know there's no place safe in this part of D.C."

Brady, preceded by his two bodyguards, each with gun drawn, inched closer.

"Stay back." Jake's unequivocal command slowed their approach.

The closest of the three, a burly man with slicked-back hair and all the charisma of a character straight out of an action-adventure movie, gestured with a lethal-looking Baretta. "What about her?"

"I'll take care of her," Jake told him succinctly. The woman still hadn't moved. He figured she was probably too damned scared.

The two lackeys glanced back at their boss for instructions. Brady hesitated, seeming to consider his
options. He stared at the crumpled form on the
pavement for several long moments.

Jake held his breath, thanking the powers that be
for the poor lighting.

"Your attention to detail leaves something to be
desired, McAlister."

"Maybe. You sure you want to discuss it now?
Who knows," Jake added mildly, knowing what he
was about to say would terminate the meeting, "she
might not be alone."

Brady sent a nervous glance around the area. A
flick of his hand motioned the others away. "We'll let
McAlister handle this," he told them decisively, adjusting the lapels of his designer suit that had to have
cost more than Jake made in two months. He pinned
Jake with a challenging look. "I'm certain he understands the importance of taking care of loose ends.
Permanently." Leaving those ominous words hanging in the air, he and his entourage swung around and
walked briskly to the foreign luxury car parked several yards down the street.

Jake watched in frustration as a year's worth of
painstaking work drove away. He didn't move until
the car had disappeared around the corner, then he
exhaled sharply. "Okay, sweetheart, on your feet.
Let's get the hell out of here."

But the woman didn't move. Suppressing his irritation, he glanced down at her. Her face was angled
away from him. In the shadows cast by the lone light
bulb at the far end of the alley, he could just make out
an egg-size lump on the back of her head, matting her
light-colored hair with blood.

Ignoring a twinge of concern, he placed his hand on her right shoulder, bared by her skimpy dress. Her skin felt clammy, and she didn't respond to his touch. Carefully he turned her head so he could get a look at her face. Great. She was unconscious. Now what? He sent a quick glance up and down the deserted street. He had precious little time to get them to safety, and the clock was ticking.

He assessed the slender, motionless form that prevented him from making a quick escape. Her clothes were too sexually suggestive, her perfume too heavy and her makeup too garish. Dollars to doughnuts her hair color came straight out of a bottle. Lord knew where she'd gotten the frizzy curls.

He shook his head. He'd dealt with enough working girls to recognize one when he saw her. But this one seemed to have wandered away from D.C.'s usual "business district."

Just how much had she seen before he'd spotted her?

She stirred restlessly and moaned. Her eyelids fluttered, then opened. For several heartbeats she looked up at him. Even in the dim light he could read her disorientation and pain, tinged with momentary terror. She struggled to sit up and grabbed her head. Cursing softly, she lay back against the cement.

"Take it easy," Jake ordered grimly. Now that she was conscious, he wanted to keep her that way.

She shook her head—whether to clear it or in response to him, he wasn't certain—and tried to sit up again. This time she succeeded.

"You okay?" Urgency made his tone curt.

She nodded, the merest movement of her head. The action reminded him of some royal family member acknowledging one of her lesser subjects. Definitely out of character, he thought wryly, for someone dressed the way she was. After a few seconds, she determinedly got to her feet. Swaying slightly, she braced herself against the nearby brick wall.

In one fluid motion, Jake rolled to stand beside her and extended a steadying hand. "Can you walk?"

She avoided his grasp. "I can walk."

And hookers have haloes. Intuition told him she wasn't going to accept his help readily, so he saved himself the hassle. Seizing her arm in a firm grip, he headed them in the opposite direction Brady's car had taken, all the while wondering if he'd end up having to carry her.

She stumbled along for several steps. "Wait a minute," she said, trying to shake free of his hold. "Where are you taking me?"

"Away from here," he told her tersely, still hustling her along beside him, giving only minimal consideration to the bump on her head.

She stopped abruptly, forcing him to stop, too.

"Now what?" he asked, barely hanging on to his patience. She was tall, almost as tall as he was, he noted, eyeing her ridiculously high spiked heels. How did anyone wear those things, much less parade up and down a cement sidewalk? Of course with her looks, he doubted she had to do much parading. He felt a stirring of masculine appreciation and immediately squelched it.

As if she'd read his thoughts, she studied him for several seconds. "Do I know you?"

"Could we dispense with the formalities until we get the hell away from here?" he countered.

But she wouldn't budge. Continuing to stare at him, she moistened her full bottom lip, heavily painted a deep red. "Do you know who I am?"

Jake knew, though for the life of him he couldn't say how, that the provocative act wasn't meant to entice. Damn, but he didn't need this. "Look, sugar," he said, no longer curbing his irritation, "we've got to get outta here. Fast. Before our friends decide to double back and check on things."

"*Our* ... friends?" she questioned.

He muttered another oath. "You know, the nice gentlemen who were showing off their hardware a few minutes ago. Remember?"

Confusion flitted across her features, then was masked. "Right," she said quickly, seeming to acquiesce. "Where to?"

Maybe he could simply leave her, he thought, but even before the idea was fully formed he discarded it. If the others did come back, there'd be hell to pay. And he had some questions to ask her. Besides, how much trouble could one groggy hooker be?

"The car's a few blocks from here. Think you can make it?"

She didn't answer, but this time when he took her arm, she didn't resist.

Her head pounded, and the acid taste of panic filled her mouth. She touched the tender spot just behind her left ear and rubbed her fingers together, relieved that the bleeding seemed to have stopped.

Her movement caught the attention of the man who was driving the nondescript sedan with alarming speed through the night-lit city streets. "You're not going to pass out on me again, are you?" he asked.

She looked directly at him for the first time since he'd unceremoniously shoved her into his car and they'd roared off. Dressed in jeans that looked as though they'd seen their best days, an old T-shirt and a black leather vest, he was the epitome of what every woman should avoid at all costs on any dark, deserted street. The twisted bandanna tied around his forehead to hold his longish hair in place and a hard jaw shadowed with a two-plus-days' growth of beard seemed to confirm her suspicion.

"Somehow I doubt 'passed out' defines what happened to me." *Knocked* out had to be more accurate. She grimaced slightly and dropped her hand back to her lap, struggling to clear her thoughts.

He chuckled, the sound coming from deep in his chest, and skimmed his gaze over her. "Right, honey. I'll rephrase the question. How do you feel?"

"My head hurts," she stated shortly. "And I don't answer to honey. Or sugar." Her offhand retort served only to increase her anxiety, since at this precise moment she wasn't certain *what* she answered to.

He shrugged. "Fair enough. The name's McAlister. And you are...?"

She wanted desperately to say, You mean you don't know? But she didn't. The question added to the others buzzing around in her head, and she tamped down the rising hysteria. She couldn't afford to lose control. The fog clouding her memory wouldn't supply answers, yet a part of her advised caution. Some instinct told her to wait, to find out first who this McAlister person was. Find out why he had rescued her. And from what.

She couldn't remember. The only thing she knew for sure was that she'd come to on the cold cement a short while ago. For now, she decided, it was probably prudent to keep that small detail to herself.

After several long moments of silence, his gaze left the road and settled on her again. "Question too tough?"

Question? Oh, yes, he'd asked for her name. "Mary," she supplied quickly, pulling a name out of thin air.

"Mary," he repeated, seeming to test it for accuracy. She was relieved when he apparently accepted it.

"Where are you taking me?"

"I'm taking *us* out of danger." He suddenly hit the brakes, jerking the wheel sharply to the right and barely avoiding a car that had run a stop sign. "I hope."

The momentum threw her to the left, and she grabbed for the nearest solid object—which happened to be one rock-hard, denim-clad thigh.

"Buckle up," he ordered tersely. "We'll have to wait on the fun and games."

She snatched her hand away and fumbled with the seat belt until she'd fastened it securely. "Wouldn't going to a police station be the logical choice?" By now they must have passed within shouting distance of several. Despising the lingering sense of confusion, she wondered how she knew that, when she couldn't seem to remember her own name.

"Not necessarily," McAlister said cryptically.

She shot him another questioning look. "Why not?"

His gaze drifted over her again. It was almost as if he'd touched her, and her skin tingled in response. "Judging by the way you're dressed, I'd say you'd want to keep a little distance between yourself and the cops.''

She ran a quick inventory of her own clothing. A black, skintight spandex minidress rode better than halfway up her thighs, which, she noted with dismay, were encased in black fishnet stockings, sporting a large tear in each knee. Her shoes were obviously made for effect, not comfort, and the effect that came to mind wasn't at all reassuring. Considering the skimpiness of her dress, why wasn't she wearing a coat against the chilly night air? She didn't want to dwell on the likely reason. He could have a point.

Again she fingered the angry bruise on the back of her head. ''A hospital, then?''

''Not a smart move.''

Her uneasiness increased. ''No?''

He waited a beat. ''Our friends could be watching the hospitals.''

There it was again—*our friends*. She wished he wouldn't keep referring to their faceless enemy in just those terms. She wished she felt brave enough to ask what made them the enemy. For that matter, she wished she felt brave enough simply to ask what had happened. But she was still too disoriented. And she was half afraid that if she started asking questions, she might give herself away before she'd fully calculated the risks.

''Fine,'' she said, keeping the apprehension from her voice with effort. ''Then let me off anywhere. I'll take it from here.''

He seemed to give serious consideration to her suggestion before shaking his head. ''Can't do that, either.''

Somehow she'd known he was going to say that. "What is it with you?" she asked, agitation making her words sarcastic. "Are you a rent-a-knight-in-shining-armor or have you appointed yourself my personal guardian angel?" Something about the question stirred a memory, but it faded before she could retrieve it. She laced her clammy-cold fingers into a tight knot to keep them from trembling.

A cynical grin curved his hard mouth—a mouth she was unaccountably certain rarely smiled. "I guarantee neither of those terms applies to me," he said softly.

She shivered. They were speeding through one of Washington's rougher neighborhoods. Even at this late hour small-time drug dealers plied their wares on the streets. And women, dressed in disturbingly similar fashion to herself, sauntered up and down the sidewalks, advertising what they had to offer. Again she felt the pull of familiarity. And panic. Who was she? Why had she been in that alley? And what had happened there?

"Do you mind telling me exactly what you *are* planning to do with me?"

"Right now? Have someone take a look at that cut."

It seemed a fairly benign objective for the moment and, judging by the pounding in her head, probably an intelligent one. Warily she settled back in her seat and concentrated on not passing out again.

At least that saved her from asking questions she wasn't sure she was ready to hear the answers to.

Jake McAlister watched as Sondra Harding set the last of three sutures in the scalp of her blond-haired patient. "There," said the older woman, helping Mary sit up. "I think that should do it."

"Thank you." Mary gripped the edge of the makeshift operating table, as if waiting for the dizziness to pass.

Jake had to be impressed. Unlike many women in his experience, Mary hadn't once flinched or made a sound while Sondra had worked on her. In fact, Mary's attitude ever since he'd rescued her was puzzling. She'd kept herself under tight control, and what little fear he'd glimpsed from time to time had been swiftly reined in. "Thanks, Sondra. I owe you one," he said.

"You owe me several," she corrected good-naturedly. "But I've stopped counting."

Sondra was somewhere in her early forties, but Jake knew hard living had aged her beyond her years. She'd been his older sister's friend, and he'd learned long ago that she was one of the handful of people he could count on. At some point in her colorful past, she'd acquired a good amount of medical knowledge. This wasn't the first time he'd used her abilities. She came from his territory, and he could trust her to discreetly handle any problem he brought her. Like this one.

Jake sent her a lopsided grin. "You're not supposed to remind me."

Sondra began putting away her medical supplies as she ran a critical eye over Mary. "You know she ought to see a doctor," she told him.

Rubbing a hand over the dark stubble covering his jaw, he expelled a deep breath. "I can't risk it."

His words made the muscles in Mary's belly rebel. The events of the past several hours were beginning to catch up with her. She wasn't sure how much longer she was going to be able to hang on to the contents of her stomach.

McAlister shoved both hands into his hip pockets and sent Sondra a penetrating look. "You think she'll be okay?"

A frown deepened the lines on the older woman's forehead. "Best I can tell. But I'd feel better if she was checked over by a professional."

"Would you two please stop acting as if I wasn't here?" Mary snapped, anxiety finally getting the better of her. "I can take care of myself, thank you very much."

McAlister studied her face. "Not at the moment you can't," he said dismissively and returned his attention to Sondra. "I need another favor."

"Name it."

"A place to stay."

"You're always welcome here," Sondra offered. "This won't be the first time it's been used as a safe house."

He nodded his appreciation. "It shouldn't be more than a few days."

"Okay. What else?"

"Someone to watch my place."

"You don't ask for much, do you?"

"I wouldn't ask if it wasn't important."

Sondra sighed philosophically. "With you, McAlister, it's always important."

"Thanks," he said, accepting her wisecrack as agreement. "Get Will to keep an ear out for any rumblings about what happened tonight. But tell him his butt's in a sling if he doesn't stay out of trouble."

"I'll give him your message," said the older woman, then turned to Mary. "Get some rest. And don't try anything creative."

Mary felt as if she should answer "Yes, ma'am" and perhaps salute.

"You," Sondra directed to McAlister, "keep that wound disinfected. And watch her. If there's any change, get in touch with me. You know where I'll be."

One side of his mouth lifted in a half smile, and he did say "Yes, ma'am."

Sondra collected a few personal things, and McAlister walked her to the front door. They spoke quickly, their voices low, making it impossible for Mary to pick up more than an occasional word or two. She wished she could hear what they were saying—or maybe she didn't. Maybe she shouldn't want to know. Whatever it was would probably frighten her even more than she already was.

Eyeing the bandanna tied around his forehead, she wondered if its colors indicated an affiliation with a gang. She tried to think objectively. He didn't act like someone who would take orders. Of course that left the possibility of his being the leader. The thought did nothing to ease her apprehension. In fact, the panic she'd managed to hold at bay so far threatened to break free. *Steady,* she warned herself.

She surveyed her surroundings, realizing that Sondra's house possibly represented her only oasis of safety for the present. It was old but clean. And small. When McAlister closed the door behind Sondra and turned to regard her with impassive eyes, she experienced an inexplicable flutter of awareness along with the sensation that more than this man's size blocked any avenue of escape she might have.

"I'd like to get cleaned up, if you don't mind," she said quickly in a bid to flee before she did something rash—like asking him to explain his earlier references to "our friends."

Chapter Two

The woman looked ready to drop, and Jake speculated just how long it would take before she gave in to the urge. She still sat rigidly on the edge of the table where Sondra had left her. She'd told him her name was Mary, but it didn't fit—it was too simple, too straightforward. He cursed softly, remembering Sondra's warning about her needing rest. "Bathroom's this way."

"Thank you," she said, her tone subdued and scrupulously polite. He directed her to the cramped room on the second floor of the row house, and she gratefully disappeared inside.

After rounding up a clean towel and one of Sondra's old sweat suits, he tapped on the door. Mary opened it cautiously. The bathroom light slanted across her face, accentuating the fact that her makeup was now badly smudged, almost as if she'd been crying. The thought unsettled him. *You're getting fanciful, McAlister.* The woman probably hadn't cried since she'd seduced her first man.

He thrust the supplies at her. "I couldn't find a toothbrush," he told her not quite apologetically.

"Thanks, I think I can improvise," she said, accepting the bundle.

"Right." He regarded her for a moment longer. "I'll check that cut again after you're finished."

Nodding, she started to close the door, but he easily blocked the move with one hand.

Her gaze jerked to his face, and she raised a questioning eyebrow. It gave her an imperious air, like someone who was used to putting people, particularly men, in their place.

"Yell," he told her firmly, "if you feel like you're going to pass out again."

"I'll be fine."

He didn't move.

"All right," she said sharply, seeming to understand he wouldn't relent until she agreed. "I'll call you."

Only then did he release his hold on the door.

As soon as she'd closed and locked the bathroom door, Mary took a deep breath, grateful to escape McAlister's overwhelming presence. She began stripping off her clothes, a growing sense of dread making her movements awkward. As she removed each piece, she carefully examined it for anything that might provide a clue to her identity.

There were no pockets. And she found no labels in any of the clothing, including her underwear. Odd. Even her shoes had no markings. Had she been carrying a purse? If so, was it still lying somewhere back there in that alley? Or had her rescuer taken it? She tried to recall if she'd noticed McAlister with anything resembling a purse. Nothing.

She looked in the badly pocked mirror above the equally scarred sink. It wasn't that she didn't recognize the reflection staring back at her, but she couldn't put a name to the face. Of course, the face looked as if the tasteless makeup had been applied with anonymity in mind. She clutched the sides of the basin to keep her hands from shaking. She needed answers, but apparently she wasn't going to find them in here. It looked as if fate had stepped in and she'd be forced to trust McAlister, whether wise or not—at least enough to ask him some pertinent questions. That, or try to find a means of escape.

She visualized the man she knew waited for her downstairs and shivered. He had the solid build of a street fighter, someone who knew how to defend himself and could do it with ease. Right now she needed protection more than freedom. And McAlister represented her best bet.

Stepping under an anemic shower, she sucked in a sharp breath as the water made contact with the strawberries on both knees. Well, she rationalized, gritting her teeth, if the cold spray didn't clear her mind, maybe the pain would. She grabbed a bar of soap and began scrubbing, then reached for a bottle of inexpensive shampoo that she found on the edge of the tub. Something told her Sondra wouldn't approve of her washing her hair, would scold her for getting the freshly sutured cut wet. But then Sondra didn't know how desperate she was to feel clean again.

A short while later she stepped out of the shower, dried off and pulled on the well-worn gray sweats. They were a decided improvement, she thought wryly, over the skintight dress she'd been wearing.

Time to face the inevitable. She followed the smell of strong coffee downstairs to the tiny kitchen. McAlister stood in front of the stove, his back to her, scrambling eggs. He handled the chore with an ease born of familiarity, but the domestic scene seemed out of character. She couldn't help speculating if his casual manner suggested he was accustomed to escaping gun-wielding men of questionable character on a regular basis.

The nervous flutter in the pit of her stomach increased alarmingly.

Jake glanced over his shoulder to find Mary poised just inside the kitchen. Taking in her wet hair, he muttered an oath and turned off the flame under the pan. In three long strides he had her by the arm, startling a protest from her.

"Why is it," she asked in irritation as he propelled her down the hallway toward the front room, "that you're continually hauling me off somewhere?"

"Because you seem to have a knack for doing stupid things?" he suggested conversationally, then grinned a feral smile that did little to take the sting out of his words.

He seated her on a chair next to the table where Sondra had tended to her head earlier. The table seemed to exist solely for this purpose, Mary decided. Sondra probably patched up wounds on a regular basis.

"Is Sondra a doctor?" Mary asked.

"No. But she knows enough about medicine not to kill you. Assuming you have enough sense to listen to what she says." He rummaged through a drawer and withdrew a bottle of hydrogen peroxide and some cotton.

She thought about simply getting up and walking away. "You certainly know how to make a woman feel better."

He gave her a sharp look, his dark expression daring her to move. "Don't you realize," he said shortly, "how easy it is for a cut like this to get infected?"

The last thing he needed was for her to get sick enough that he'd be forced to take her to a hospital. Hospitals asked questions, just like the police. He couldn't chance either one.

"I'm capable of making decisions concerning my personal hygiene."

"Yeah, I can tell. Now hold still," he ordered. Steadying her head against his stomach, he sifted through her hair. The strands had begun to dry, and he noticed the frizziness was gone. It felt silky in his hands, touchable. Finding the injured area, he gently swabbed it with a cotton ball soaked in disinfectant, while absently wondering when cheap shampoo had started smelling delicious.

Jake inspected the wound for damage. The stitches were still in place, he noted with relief, the edges tightly closed. He also noted the absence of any dark roots mixed in with the honey-blond color. Either she'd recently used a bottle of bleach, or... No, even he knew that bleach couldn't produce the infinite shades of gold glimmering in her hair. Another man might overlook something that minor. But he wouldn't. Survival had trained him to notice and file away even insignificant details.

"What possessed you to wash your hair, for God's sake?" Having suffered through countless stitches himself during his lifetime, he knew the dangers, but even more he knew how badly a fresh cut could hurt. It amazed him that she would have voluntarily put her head under water.

For all the man's anger, Mary couldn't help noticing that his touch was exceptionally gentle. Would a member of a gang be this careful? The errant thought made her feel that much more off balance.

With her face pressed so intimately against the abrasive fabric of his jeans, Mary was surrounded by McAlister's distinct scent. That, along with his gentle hands, challenged her shaky self-control. She felt hated moisture well up in her eyes. "Look, stop fussing over me. I can take care of myself," she stated, not for the first time tonight, and eased her hand up to angrily swipe at the tears. How did she explain to him that making this simple decision had given her a sense of control over at least one portion of a world that had suddenly turned alien?

Jake moved back a half step and lifted Mary's chin to examine her face. Her eyes were the most extraordinary shade of green he'd ever encountered, her tears transforming them into glittering emeralds. For an instant she looked totally defenseless. It didn't jibe. And it made him suspicious.

"Somehow I didn't take you for the type to use tears."

She jerked away from his grasp. "I'm not," she snapped, uncertain whether her assertion was accurate. She drew herself up straighter on the chair, gathering her forces. "I'm just tired. Do you mind?"

He experienced a surge of admiration. "I won't argue it hasn't been quite a night." He continued to study her. How could someone this beautiful be mixed up in prostitution? But then again, he reminded himself, that hadn't stopped his sister.

Years ago he'd ceased trying to second-guess what made people tick and learned simply to accept their foibles. He'd found life a helluva lot less painful that way. If he didn't expect much, he wasn't likely to be disappointed. Still, his training told him that something about this woman didn't quite add up.

"Worst night in memory," she agreed with irony.

"Tell me something."

Mary eyed him warily. "If I can."

"What were you doing in the alley tonight?"

She stood abruptly and pushed past him, trying to suppress the sinking feeling in the pit of her stomach. If he had to ask, then it meant he didn't know. She chose her words carefully. "I could ask you the same thing."

"You could." He replaced the bottle of peroxide and closed the drawer. Turning to face her, he rested his hips against the edge of the table and folded his arms across his chest. "And we could spend what's left of the night playing games."

She scowled at him, but the wry curl to his smile told her he knew she was stalling. She began to pace.

He didn't push for an answer; he could wait. He was good at waiting. What a waste, he thought, watching Mary prowl the room. She should have been a model. She had the looks and the height. But then, so had Debbie. Thinking of his sister even now caused a deep ache in his chest. Was this woman into drugs, too? Somehow he doubted it.

While Sondra had worked on Mary, he'd covertly checked her arms for needle tracks and found none. Of course, he knew only too well that the marks could be hidden in very imaginative places. And there were drugs that didn't leave visible signs. But he sensed an innate pride in this woman usually absent in a druggie.

In any case, he'd know soon enough. Like it or not, he was sure she was going to be with him for a while. At least until he figured out what to do with her. No way in hell could he risk letting her walk away until he'd figured out who she was. And how much she'd seen earlier tonight.

Mary winced and stopped pacing as the scrapes on her knees protested the subtle abrasion from her sweatpants.

"What's wrong?" Jake asked, noticing her grimace.

"I think my knees may have taken a worse beating than my head."

He straightened away from the table. "Let's have a look."

"Don't worry about it," she said quickly. She wasn't certain her fragile nerves could stand another exposure to McAlister's brand of gruff gentleness quite so soon.

He sighed and pinned her with a direct stare. "Is everything with you a hassle?"

"Do you always issue orders?" she retorted, but she walked gingerly back to the chair and sat down. Her knees needed tending, and refusing his offer would be petty—and not very smart.

"It seems to be the only way I can get you to co-operate," he said wryly, hunkering down in front of her and reaching for her right leg. Her feet were bare except for the brilliant red polish on her toenails. He carefully raised one pant leg, surprised to find such incredibly smooth, lightly tanned skin. His reaction to it surprised him even more.

Something nagged at him. There was a well-cared-for look about her, down to her neatly manicured toes, that seemed to dispute his initial suspicions about her. He didn't pretend to be an expert on women's fashions, but even he recognized subtle quality when he saw it, quality not usually found in a streetwalker's wardrobe. And she lacked the typical rough-around-the-edges, worn-out-before-her-time look of other hookers he'd known. Scrubbed clean of makeup, she appeared softer, almost fragile. Even in Sondra's old sweats, she was still unbelievably sexy.

Still? The word rattled against the edge of his self-control. He hadn't been aware he'd thought of her as sexy in the first place.

Prostitutes had never held any interest for him in the past. Why should this one be different? Damn, he needed to get his mind back on the current problem—which was what to do about this woman.

When he uncovered the angry scrape marring her right knee, he whistled softly and looked up at her. "You hiding any more secrets?" he asked.

Other than the fact that she could remember nothing personal about herself prior to a handful of hours ago? She wished to heaven she knew. "You don't like secrets?" she prevaricated.

He held her gaze. "Depends on the secret."

She decided it was probably a mistake to try fencing with this man. "This one—" she indicated the knee he still held gently in one strong hand "—is part of a matched set."

He searched her face for several seconds longer until Mary was forced to look away. Out of the corner of her eye she saw him open the tube of ointment and gently rub the medication on both knees, then cover them with large bandages. He slowly pulled down each pant leg, again assessing her.

His eyes were ice blue, sharp. Mary experienced a quiver of sexual awareness and instantly suppressed it. It had to be his pure masculine strength, she told herself, and the fact that tonight she badly needed to draw from it. But even as she tried to reassure herself, she knew intuitively that this wasn't customary for her.

She wanted information, she reminded herself, and she wasn't going to find out very much if she remained uncooperative. Or maybe it was simply desperation that drove her to follow his lead, even at the risk of being incautious. She nervously tucked a strand of shoulder-length hair behind her ear. "I'm the one who got knocked in the head, so what happened tonight's a bit...fuzzy." And the fuzziness seemed to be increasing by the minute, she observed uneasily. "Would you mind filling in some of the blanks?"

Either she was being completely candid, Jake reflected skeptically, or very clever. After what she'd been through, it *was* conceivable that a lot of what had gone down tonight could be hazy. He'd give her that. Okay, he'd play it her way for a while and see where she took him. "Fair enough." He straightened to his full height. "Where do you want me to start?"

She left her seat again to put some distance between them. "Oh, someplace obvious," she said. "Like how the heck I got this lump on my head."

He began clearing away the medical supplies for the second time. "You can blame me for that."

"You?" She looked at him sharply. "How?"

"You must've gotten it when I tackled you."

"Tackled?"

He nodded, and she thought she detected just a spark of mischief. It eased her anxiety the tiniest bit.

"Why would you tackle me?"

He sobered. "To keep you from getting shot."

A shudder crept up her spine. "Courtesy of... our friends?"

Again he nodded.

She resumed her pacing, grateful for the padding he'd placed over the scrapes on her knees. "Who are they, McAlister?"

"People you don't want to tangle with," he said evenly.

She digested this. "But you do."

"Oh, yeah," he drawled. "You can depend on it."

Something in the very softness of his tone sent a new wave of goose bumps scurrying along her arms, and she absently rubbed her hands over the sleeves of her borrowed sweatshirt. "But why would they want to shoot me?"

He hesitated, then shrugged. "Maybe to scare you away. You were in the wrong place at the wrong time."

Fear increased the pounding in her head. "You mean like I am right now?"

"Right now you're in the safest place, under the circumstances."

Tell me what those circumstances are, she wanted to shout. "What if someone's looking for me?" With effort she managed to make the suggestion sound nonchalant.

"Is there?" he countered, as if they were discussing something as innocuous as the possibility of rain.

In answer she lifted one shoulder noncommittally, since anything else would give away her secret—she didn't have a clue. Was there someone who would miss her, come looking for her? The hollow feeling inside her expanded, invading all the dark places where her personal memories should be.

He closed the distance between them, once more imposing his commanding presence on her, making her acknowledge his greater strength. And she had no doubt that it was deliberate. "How about you answering some questions for me?"

The urge was strong to tell him that he hadn't yet come close to satisfying her own curiosity—that she still had dozens of questions. She backed up a half step. Could she trust him? she wondered, trying to calm her galloping heartbeat. But, a rational part of her argued, hadn't he already proven himself tonight? He'd rescued her from a dangerous situation—at least that's what he'd implied. He'd had her injuries tended to—*that* she knew for a fact. And he was protecting her now. Didn't that indicate he could be trusted? But what it came down to was, did she have a choice?

She sighed. He was the lesser of two evils. Better the devil she knew than the devil she didn't. "I'll try."

Satisfaction softened his features. "What brought you to that alley tonight?"

"I wish I could give you an answer." She took a deep breath, squared her shoulders and looked him straight in the eye. "But I can't. You see, I don't know. In fact, I don't have the vaguest idea who I am, or what happened before I woke up."

Chapter Three

Jake stared at her for long seconds, his expression watchful. "You don't remember anything?"

"I know what year it is. I know who's president. I seem to be able to remember all sorts of useless information." Mary spread her arms, conveying her sense of helplessness. "But I can't seem to remember anything about *me.*"

"There are times when that kind of memory lapse could have real advantages." He made no effort to hide his skepticism. "In fact, a person might even consider it a blessing."

"Perhaps."

She attempted a smile, but something Jake couldn't name darkened her eyes. Intuitively he knew his not-so-subtle accusation didn't apply to her. He felt the first stirring of sympathy and ruthlessly pushed it aside. She was simply a problem—one he had to figure out the best way to handle. He didn't give a damn, he told himself firmly, about her emotional well-being.

"I need coffee." What he really needed was to put some distance between himself and this woman. "And you need something to eat."

"No food." The mere suggestion had Mary's stomach performing flip-flops. "But coffee sounds great," she said, wondering as she followed him back to the tiny kitchen if she took cream or sugar or drank it black.

While Jake reheated the eggs and made toast, she poured two mugs of coffee and got out the meager eating utensils. Once they were seated, he asked, "You didn't find any ID on you?"

"No." Mary took a swallow of the bitter liquid, grimaced and went to the ancient refrigerator in search of milk.

"Nothing in your pockets? Credit card, match-book, a note?"

She slid back into her chair and cautiously tasted her coffee. Better, she decided and took several sips, the strong brew momentarily steadying her nerves. "I went through everything. Meticulously. There was nothing, not even a label."

"Interesting that you'd think to check labels," he reflected.

She shrugged. "Don't all women look at labels?" She didn't tell him that it had seemed the logical thing to do, that even as she'd done it, she'd sensed it wasn't for the trivial reason of checking out designers. But for the life of her, she couldn't say why.

"I've never given it much thought."

"You know, you're very good at asking questions about me." She set down her mug, holding it loosely within the circle of her hands, allowing its heat to warm her. "But you haven't told me very much about yourself. I don't even know if McAlister is your first or last name. If I didn't know better, I'd swear you were a cop."

To someone not watching him closely, she doubted the stiffening of his shoulders would have been perceptible. He drained the last of his coffee, then carefully replaced his mug on the table. "Considering what you've just told me, how would you know?" he asked, easily sidestepping.

Good question. And she didn't have an answer. It had been a gut-level guess. The shadow of a memory surfaced, only to fade again, and her hands tightened around the mug in frustration. "You're right, of course." To distract herself, she went to retrieve the coffeepot, brought it to the table and refilled their cups. "Did you happen to notice if I had a purse with me when you rescued me?"

He shoved his plate aside, impatient with himself for not thinking of that. "I was pretty busy just getting us out of there before someone got shot. So, no, I didn't notice." This seemed to be his night for mistakes, the first being that he'd somehow overlooked this woman's presence until it had been too late.

Maybe he should make a quick trip back to the alley and check things out. But first he needed to find out what information Mary could provide. "Okay, let's take this one step at a time. What *do* you remember?"

Searching through the mist that still clouded her mind, Mary absently picked up a slice of toast off his plate and broke it in half. "Hearing voices."

"Recall what they said?"

Keenly aware of Jake's intense scrutiny, she replayed the fuzzy scene in her mind's eye, disheartened when she couldn't focus it. It was as if she were trying to see a movie through a thick fog. She could glimpse snatches of it but not enough to discern anything clearly. She shook her head. "The words were disjointed and didn't make a lot of sense. But I have the impression that whoever was talking was angry."

Jake grunted. If indeed she *had* lost her memory, how long, he wondered, before it would return and how much would she eventually remember? Logically, he knew she couldn't have seen too much. He was good at his job. If she'd been there for very long, he would've known. Which made her getting past him in the first place even more irritating—not to mention embarrassing. Dammit, who was she? Was she a threat? To him? To his operation?

Dressed in Sondra's old sweats she looked... comfortable—certainly not a threat. At least, he thought wryly, not the variety he'd been worrying about earlier. "Anything else?"

"I remember opening my eyes and seeing you."

A smile played at one side of his mouth and his eyes warmed with humor. "That must have been some shock."

It was the first genuine smile McAlister had offered her, and it set off warning sirens in her head—along with effervescent bubbles of awareness in her stomach. This man could be disarming when he wanted. Even as her own lips responded, she cautioned herself not to let her guard down. "Must have been."

He continued studying her for the space of several heartbeats. "The name's Jake McAlister," he said, finally giving her his full name.

"Hello, Jake McAlister." With a dramatic flourish, she extended her hand just as if this were their first meeting. "Sorry I can't return the introduction."

The tiny lines around his eyes deepened. "I didn't think Mary suited you."

She was acutely aware of the strength in the hand that grasped hers. It radiated warmth and unshakable determination. Her smile slipped, and she pulled her hand free.

"It was the first name that came to mind." The most disturbing loss in all this, she was coming to realize, was her name. A name was such a personal thing. Not knowing it made her feel like a nonentity... almost as if she'd never existed.

Jake sensed her momentary anguish, and her withdrawal left his palm feeling oddly empty. Against his better judgment, this woman roused a long-forgotten protective instinct in him—something he hadn't allowed himself to feel since Debbie died. Damn, but he didn't want this. What in hell was he going to do with a woman who had amnesia? The only reason he was keeping her with him, he reminded himself, was that her life was in danger and he felt responsible.

Hell, he *was* responsible. If he hadn't slipped up on something as basic as clearing an area of civilians before an operation went down, she wouldn't be in this predicament.

But that didn't explain why he accepted everything she'd told him as truth. Maybe it was because he hadn't been prepared for such openness. Telling a complete stranger, a stranger she'd met under at best unusual circumstances, that she didn't know who she was had to take an incredible amount of courage. Nor was he prepared for his awakening empathy. Why, for a man who'd run from memories most of his life, did the fact that this woman had lost hers make him hurt for her?

"Hey, don't look so down." The husky sound of his voice irritated him, and he deliberately added a note of mockery. "We can come up with another name."

She folded her arms and pursed her lips. "And I'll just bet you have a suggestion."

"Yeah," he said, finding it a little unsettling that he preferred her stubbornness to her sadness. "Something haughty and sophisticated. Maybe with a regal sound to it."

She sent him a dubious look. "Such as?"

"Well, my first impulse is to shoot straight for the top. Start with Your Highness or Duchess. But under the circumstances, maybe we should go for something a little less . . . showy."

"As long as it's not sugar or honey," she muttered darkly.

His smile returned. "You don't believe I can be any more creative than that?"

She raised a challenging eyebrow.

"How about Helen?"

Strangely, the name didn't appeal to her. "Why Helen?"

His gaze roamed over her face, slowly touching on each feature, as if seeking the truth. "Helen of Troy," he finally said. "With a face like yours, the name fits." He abruptly returned his attention to the mug he kept toying with.

"Why do I think I've been insulted?" Mary wondered aloud, while wondering silently why his familiarity with the classic tale should surprise her. It was just one more contradiction to add to all the others surrounding this man.

She was very beautiful, Jake acknowledged again, and very dangerous. He recalled all the problems she'd caused him in the brief time he'd known her. Like Helen, she had the kind of beauty that could make a man do foolish things. And like Paris before him, Jake was probably setting himself up for unwitting betrayal. "Yeah, definitely Helen."

"Thanks all the same, but I think I'll stick with Mary." She sent him a blinding smile, one she was aware was artificial, one she was certain she'd used often in the past. The thought wasn't consoling. "So," she said, "where does this leave us?"

Jake focused on Mary's mouth. It was full and naked and vulnerable. And kissable. She was already weaving a spell. He felt the unmistakable tightening low in his gut and silently cursed, wondering if she was half as aware of him as he was of her. Or if he was simply engaging in dangerous fantasies. Either way it meant trouble. "Good question."

What the hell was he going to do about her? He shifted uncomfortably in his chair. He might feel responsible for her, but, he reminded himself grimly, he hadn't been able to keep his own sister safe. What made him think he could do any better job with this woman? And bottom line, he couldn't keep her with him indefinitely. She might be shook up now, but sooner or later, memory or no, she'd demand he let her go. He could stall her for a while, but time was running out.

Besides, all this concern for her was making him jumpy. He'd trained himself a lifetime ago not to allow anyone past his guard. He did what had to be done—and he didn't get emotionally involved.

She was a hindrance, keeping him from getting back to the more pressing problem of George Brady. Jake had an ongoing operation he had to salvage. He couldn't afford to let anything—or anyone—interfere with it, not at this critical stage.

Mary cleared her throat. "I guess this means you didn't know me before our rather...unusual meeting."

"No."

The earlier fuzziness had turned into a headache, which began to pound in earnest. "Have you ever seen me before? Do you know anything about me?"

He shook his head. "Not before tonight."

Her disappointment settled like a weight in her chest. "What was I doing when you first saw me?"

"Hiding behind some boxes."

She digested that. "What were you doing?"

He shifted again in his chair. "Talking business."

"Business?"

"That's what I said."

"What kind of business?"

He studied her for a long moment. "For now that's all you need to know."

His statement was condescending, and it riled her. "Ah," she said with facetious understanding. "In other words, be a good little girl and don't ask about things that don't concern you?''

A slow, cynical smile curved his mouth, and he leaned back in his chair. "Now, that's *not* what I said."

"No, but it's what you meant." Irritation tinged her words. She got up from the table and walked across the small room to stare out the window above the sink. It overlooked a dingy, narrow walkway barely visible in the predawn light. The view, if it could be called that, consisted of a too-close boarded-up window in the next building. She turned to face him, her hands gripping the counter behind her. "Then tell me this."

"Depends on what you want to know."

"Who are you, Jake McAlister?"

She was persistent, Jake conceded. He'd known she'd get around to this question again sooner or later. "That's a pretty broad subject."

"Broad, maybe, but not ambiguous."

"What do you want to know?"

Fury and frustration at his stonewalling narrowed her eyes. She crossed her arms under her breasts, grappling with the dizziness that was steadily increasing. "Rather than continue this farce, why don't I leave now? That way I can find the answers for myself."

Jake stood so quickly that his chair crashed against the wall. In two strides he had her by the arm in a grip that said he half expected her to vanish before his eyes. "Look, lady—" he made the term sound like an insult "—the less you know about me, the better off both of us will be." His voice was deadly quiet. "I've spent most of tonight keeping you alive. In case it's not clear yet, those guys back there want you dead. If you leave, they just might get their wish.''

"Dead?" she echoed, shaking off his hand. She struggled to control the fresh fear coiling through her, the buzzing in her ears threatening to drown out all other sound.

"If you recall, that's why I had you flat on your back last night." Jake didn't want to admit that he found the sudden drain of color from her face alarming, but he couldn't afford to back off.

He was so close that Mary could see the anger freezing his eyes to ice. In sharp contrast, she was aware of the heat radiating from the solid bulk of him. A tiny voice warned her she was losing the battle for composure. "All the more reason to let me go. Obviously I'm putting you in danger." She tried one more desperate tack. "If you can't or won't help me, then you have to let me go—you have to let me try to help myself."

She looked fierce and vulnerable all at the same time. It was a potent combination, and Jake hated the effect it was having on him. He didn't want to think of her as a person with feelings, someone who could hurt, someone *he* could hurt.

"Let me spell it out for you, Helen of Troy. You're not going anywhere. The only reason you're not dead," he said through clenched teeth, "is because the vultures back there in that alley expect me to take care of it."

This time she didn't fight the blackness closing in on her. Instead, she allowed herself to fall into its welcoming oblivion.

Chapter Four

Angry voices, familiar and close, pulled Mary back to consciousness. She surfaced in murky increments, wariness telling her to keep her eyes closed and remain motionless until she identified where she was and who was talking.

"Dammit, I told you to make sure she rested," said a brusque feminine voice. "Scaring her into unconsciousness was not what I had in mind."

Sondra Harding. Recognition and relief flooded through Mary. Would someone who'd gone to the trouble of stitching up the cut in her head become a threat? Mary doubted it. Still she kept quiet, trying to orient herself, wondering how long she'd been out. She had to be lying on a bed, she decided, probably Sondra's, and Sondra was sitting beside her. The scrape of what sounded like boots on the wooden floor told her that someone heavier and probably stronger than Sondra was also in the room. And had moved closer.

"Can the lecture, Sondra. Just tell me if she'll be all right."

Mary had heard that voice before. In the alley... and later... *Jake McAlister*. She tried to control her involuntary shiver. *"The only reason you're not dead is because the vultures back there in that alley expect me to take care of it."* Her heartbeat increased alarmingly as his last words exploded into memory.

"How the hell should I know?" Sondra snapped, and Mary felt the cool touch of fingers against the pulse in her neck. "She's been out for hours, and I'm not a..." Sondra's words dwindled away. "Mary?"

Mary realized she'd been found out. Cautiously, she opened her eyes to find Sondra's worried face over her. Her gaze skittered past Sondra to collide with Jake's expressionless one.

Jake saw the momentary fear flare in her eyes, but Mary didn't look away from him. Instead, she visibly reined it in. Again he felt the tug of admiration. He'd told her enough to scare her spitless, yet her determination not to let him intimidate her was clear. She had spunk.

For the first time in memory the temptation to tell someone—specifically this woman—the truth about himself was almost irresistible.

"You should've waited a few seconds longer before you passed out on me," Jake told her, a sardonic note in his voice.

"Jake," Sondra said, a warning note in hers.

"I need to talk to her." He glanced meaningfully at Sondra. "Alone."

Sondra huffed her disapproval. "Oh, all right." She patted Mary's arm in reassurance, and the mattress shifted as the older woman stood. "But I'm warning you, Jake McAlister, don't upset her again."

He sent her a wry look. "I'll do my best."

As Sondra left the room, Mary scooted into a sitting position and leaned back against the headboard, relieved that the dizziness had subsided marginally. The sunlight filtering through the bedroom window told her it was late afternoon. She *had* been out for quite some time. "You have something to say?"

He raised an eyebrow. "You sure you're up to hearing it?"

"Hey," she parried, "if I'm going to get killed, I'd like as many details as possible."

His eyes glittered dangerously. "Dammit, I'm not going to kill you."

Mary was startled by the flood of relief that washed over her before she brought herself up short. Why in heaven's name should she believe any assurances this man gave her? "No?" She was careful to keep any sign of apprehension from her voice. "As I recall, you were pretty specific about being expected to get the job done."

"Expectation is one thing. Execution is something else again."

She suppressed another shiver. "Did you have to use that particular term?"

He expelled a heavy breath and moved a few feet away. "Look," he said, "I'm not going to hurt you."

"You said—"

"I said they *expected* me to do it."

"Am I missing something here?"

"Unless there's a damned good reason, I'm not much into doing what's expected."

She didn't have any trouble believing that. "I see."

"Do you?" He walked over to the closed door, bracing one arm against the jamb, as if he wanted access to a quick escape route. "I'd appreciate it if you'd keep it to yourself. I don't usually advertise the fact."

Was that a hint of amusement she detected? She mentally shook herself. "So that explains why you had to bring me here in the first place." And certainly explained why he wasn't impatient to let her go. He couldn't very well have someone who was supposed to be dead turn up on the streets all too alive.

"I knew you were sharp."

"And if they discover you haven't taken care of the problem—namely me," she said in comprehension, "they're not going to be pleased."

He hesitated a beat, gauging her reaction. "Something like that."

"Which puts you in danger. Therefore," she continued, putting more pieces together, "the sooner you get rid of me, so to speak, the better."

He eyed her, feeling as if she were toying with a live grenade. "You're not going anywhere until I find out who you are." She'd figured out only part of the problem. It was the rest of it that held potential disaster.

"Well, then," Mary said, "since my memory doesn't seem to want to cooperate, maybe we should try to locate my purse." She swung her legs over the side of the mattress, relieved when the room remained stationary.

"Where do you think you're going?"

"Back to where all this started." Her tone implied the answer was obvious. "Where else?"

He muttered an oath. "Do you think Sondra's going to let you out of here after what just happened? You were out cold for hours."

She looked up at him in amusement. "Why, Jake McAlister, don't tell me you're concerned about my welfare."

"Hell, no. I'm concerned about my own," he told her succinctly. "You're staying here. If anyone's going after that damned purse, it'll be me."

Feeling the need to be on a more equal footing with this man, Mary stood, and wooziness threatened her shaky equilibrium. She braced her legs against the bed, waiting for the sensation to pass. "I'm going, Jake. Please don't try to stop me."

Something told Jake he'd be wasting his time if he did. Without those ridiculous shoes of hers, she was several inches shorter than he was. Those missing inches and Sondra's baggy sweats might make her look defenseless, but neither one diminished her defiance. "Dammit, things could get dangerous."

One side of her mouth turned up in a small smile. "How much worse can they get?"

He didn't want to think about that. Hell. Maybe it would be better if he took her along. At least he could keep an eye on her. With his luck, if he left her here, she'd probably be gone before he got back.

Besides, she was beginning to have a very disturbing effect on him. The sooner he found out who she was, the sooner he could be rid of her for good. The trip back to the alley might jog her memory. And who knew, maybe she'd be useful. He certainly needed all the help he could get. Still, on a gut level, he knew taking her back to the alley was not a smart move. It could prove deadly to them both.

A noise from the downstairs cut off their debate. Jake moved swiftly across the room to an old battered bureau, jerked open a drawer and extracted a gun. Sliding it into the waistband of his jeans at the small of his back, he glanced at Mary. "I guess it wouldn't do me any good to tell you to stay put?"

She grinned at him. "Good guess, McAlister."

He muttered an oath. "Stay behind me," he growled. "Understand?"

Mary didn't argue, amazed that it felt perfectly natural for her to take this risk. As she followed Jake out into the hall and down the stairs, her pulse pounded in her ears and her senses came to full alert. She could hear Sondra speaking to someone in a low tone. Though the visitor's voice was equally low, it sounded male, and young. She saw Jake visibly relax. Mary expelled a breath and followed suit.

She entered the room at the front of the small row house one step behind Jake. Sondra and a tall adolescent male immediately stopped talking.

"Well," Sondra said, carefully inspecting Mary. "I see Jake managed to keep from inflicting more damage on you. Or maybe you've just learned how to survive."

Mary smiled wryly. "A little of both, I think."

Sondra chuckled. "Good girl." She glanced at Jake. "Your buddy here," she said, indicating the teenager standing beside her, "has something to tell you, so I'll leave you people to talk."

As Sondra left the room, Mary became conscious of the boy leisurely checking her over from head to toe. She estimated him to be somewhere in his mid-teens, but judging from the look he was giving her, she suspected he wanted people to think he was older. He let out a low, appreciative whistle.

Jake scowled and hooked an arm around the teenager's neck, pulling him into a headlock. She sensed the gruff affection in the tussle.

"Willie here is sixteen going on thirty," Jake said, feigning a right jab to his belly. "Sometimes he doesn't remember his manners."

Grinning, the boy artfully deflected the blow. "Don't call me Willie."

Jake released him. "Then watch yourself." The teasing had left his voice.

Hurt and embarrassment flickered in the youth's eyes, then quickly disappeared. "I didn't mean nothing, Jake."

Jake's son? she wondered, then discarded the idea. The coloring wasn't right, the bone structure too dissimilar. Still, he treated the boy with the easy familiarity of a parent. Or someone who cared. "Ignore Jake," she said to the teenager. "He has a bad habit of coming up with names people don't particularly care for. What would you like to be called?"

A blush stained his cheeks. "Will."

"Hi, Will," she said, biting the inside of her mouth to stifle a grin. "I'm Mary."

He stuck his hands into the pockets of his baggy pants, his own grin becoming self-conscious. "Hi."

"You keeping your nose clean, kid?" Jake interjected.

Will pulled his gaze away from Mary and made a face, clearly no more enthusiastic at being called a kid. "Yeah."

Even to her ears, his answer lacked conviction. Jake propped his shoulder against the wall. It was the same casual stance she'd seen him take before, but Mary sensed the renewed watchfulness that never entirely left him.

"Remember what we talked about?" Jake asked Will.

"I remember."

"No drugs? I don't want to get a call from the morgue to come ID your body," Jake added gruffly.

"He—" Will broke off and glanced at Mary. "Heck no, man!" he said with youthful indignity. "You can check if you want."

Jake nodded in satisfaction. "No gangs?"

The boy's features clouded for a moment. "I'm cool, man."

Mary felt more than saw Jake's doubt, tinged with concern and something more—disappointment. The muscle in his jaw tightened, but she sensed that while he might want to, Jake wouldn't pursue the issue now. She wondered, somewhat dismayed, when she'd become so adept at reading this man.

"Do you have anything worth telling me?" he asked Will.

"I did like you said." It was plain Will was trying to make amends. "I asked around if anybody'd seen a knockout chick."

Jake folded his arms across his chest, pinning the boy with a look that would send most grown men running for cover. "I told you to *listen,*" he said softly. "I didn't say anything about talking. We agreed, didn't we? You were going to stop taking stupid risks."

Will stood his ground, but his belligerent, slightly crestfallen expression made him appear younger than his sixteen years and suddenly a little lost. "I was careful, Jake. I swear."

"Wrong," Jake told him flatly. "Careful is following my instructions, dead-on."

"I was just trying to help!"

"You want to help? Do what I tell you."

The boy shoved his hands deeper into his pockets and hunched his shoulders defensively.

Jake let out a sigh and rubbed the back of his neck. "Okay," he finally said, relenting. "Tell me what you found out."

For a moment Mary thought Will might not answer. She couldn't miss Jake's concern for the boy, but she wasn't certain it was as clear to Will. This wasn't just some kid off the street to Jake. She wondered if Jake had any idea what his actions revealed about himself.

"Word on the street is a—" Will hesitated and his gaze darted to Mary "—lady looking like her's been hanging around hooker turf."

Out of the corner of his eye, Jake watched Mary stiffen, and he silently swore. He was beginning to realize she didn't much care for the possibility of her being a prostitute. For that matter, he was finding *he* didn't much care for it, either. "Did you get a name?"

"Sorry," Will said.

"At least you had sense enough not to ask," Jake muttered. "Anything else?"

The boy shuffled uncomfortably and shrugged. "Just that she's been taking care of business for a few days."

Mary smarted as one more piece of evidence dropped into place. Was it possible? Could she be a prostitute? She didn't *feel* like one. But then again, how was a prostitute supposed to feel? Desperation clawed at her stomach, and the impulse to return to the alley to search for anything that would contradict the mounting evidence almost had her rushing out the door.

Jake had heard more than he wanted. The urge to spare Mary's feelings caught him by surprise. "Any rumblings about what happened last night?" he asked, moving to the next topic and away from his troubling thoughts.

"Word is those guys ain't too happy."

Jake tensed. "Why?"

"Because no—" his voice faltered "—stiff's turned up yet."

"They should realize," Jake muttered with dark humor, "if I'd done a good job, the 'stiff' would never turn up."

Damn. He'd been afraid of this. Jake watched the small amount of color drain from Mary's face. Frowning, he dragged a hand over his rough jaw. Time was running out. Discovering Mary's identity had become critical. She was safe here for the moment, but not indefinitely. "Anything else?"

Will shook his head, looking worried. "Did I do okay?"

"Yeah," Jake told him. "You did fine."

He brightened immediately. "You want me to see what else I can dig up?" he asked eagerly.

"No," Jake said sharply, then tempered his tone. "You've done enough." He walked over to the boy and placed a hand on his shoulder, his expression softening. "What I want you to do now is look after Sondra. Okay?"

"You got it," Will assured him. Though he tried to hide it, his pleasure that Jake had once again entrusted him with responsibility was obvious.

"I'm counting on you to see that she's safe."

"I'll take care of her," Will assured him, and headed toward the back of the house to find Sondra. Almost out of the room, he stopped and turned back to Mary. "I—" He hesitated, again flustered. "Those guys, they don't know what they're talking about, you know? Don't pay no attention to them. Nobody's proved nothing yet. You don't have to worry. Jake'll take care of things."

With effort Mary held her fear to a manageable level. "I appreciate the encouragement," she said, a lump tightening her throat. She'd noted with misgiving how little regard Will showed for his own safety. He was out on the streets associating with God only knew what, and yet here he was worrying about her feelings and trying to reassure her.

A stain darkened Will's cheeks. "Sure," he said, and shrugged. "No problem."

Where was his family? she wondered, as she watched him hurry from the room. And why weren't they looking out for him? She shuddered and quickly revised the estimation of his age. He was more than sixteen going on thirty—it had to be closer to 130. She was relatively certain the things this youngster had witnessed in his short life would age even a hardened criminal. The thought made her current problems pale in comparison.

Though Jake did a good job hiding it, she knew he was concerned about Will. There was a firmness in the way he handled the kid that spoke of discipline and high expectations, but there was an underlying bond, too.

She was certain Jake was utterly unaware of that bond.

Chapter Five

"Your friend is quite a character," Mary said to Jake after Sondra left with Will.

"Sondra?"

"No. I was referring to Will."

Giving a dismissive shrug, Jake removed the automatic from his waistband and placed it on the nearby table. "He's just a smart-mouthed kid."

"Really? Seems you're awfully concerned about 'just a smart-mouthed kid.'"

A scowl came and went on Jake's features. "Strictly self-preservation."

"I see."

"Do you?" The need to justify himself was irritating. He never offered explanations for his actions. "In this part of town, too many kids choose to become victimizers rather than waiting around to become victims," he nonetheless found himself telling her. "If I can keep the kid from taking that route, maybe he won't try to kill me some dark night."

She wondered if he realized how weak his explanation was. Or how transparent. Her intuition was right. Jake didn't want to acknowledge that Will meant something to him. That, or he didn't want anyone to know. If she had to make a bet, her money would be on both. She again found it astonishing and somewhat disturbing that she was beginning to read Jake so easily. Was this a side effect of having a mind uncluttered by her own memories or preconceptions?

"Ah. You're saying you don't have a soft spot for Will."

An emotion Jake didn't care to name surfaced briefly before he relegated it to a dark corner of his mind. "I'll give you some good advice," he said, walking over to a small closet across the room—away from the woman who seemed to have a talent for getting under his skin. "Soft people don't make it in my world." He didn't mention that believing that left a person empty inside, or that he'd found over time that empty was preferable to the alternative. If he was empty, there couldn't be any pain.

"Maybe you're right," she said, her words following him into the closet. "But without some softness, I'm not certain I'd *want* to make it."

Her wistful remark echoed inside him. Was she speaking from experience? Had there been softness in her life? Did she have a family? A husband? Someone special?

He didn't like what that last thought did to his gut. Why should he care one way or the other if there was anyone special in her life? Shoving aside several items on the closet shelf with more force than necessary, he reminded himself again that he didn't want to get emotionally tangled up with her. He unlocked a small compartment and retrieved a box of ammunition and several extra clips. When he started back to the table, he noticed his gun in Mary's hand and froze.

Instinct told him to seize the weapon immediately, but something about her intense concentration restrained him. He studied her as she hefted the Colt easily in her right hand, gauging the balance. She checked the safety, released the clip and set it aside, then pulled back on the slide to eject the .45 caliber shell from the chamber. Keeping her thumbs well away from the recoil mechanism, she wrapped both hands around the handle, aimed at a point on the far wall and sighted down the barrel. It was as flawless a demonstration of gun procedure as any he'd seen executed by professionals.

Jake let out a silent whistle. Now, he could buy the idea that the average prostitute might have a nodding acquaintance with guns. But gun procedure like a pro? Not likely. To handle a gun this well required extensive training. And where would someone from this part of town go to acquire that level of expertise?

How many other secrets was she hiding? Soundlessly, he moved up behind her until only inches separated them. "It pulls a little to the left," he told her, keeping his voice quiet. "I haven't gotten around to adjusting it."

She jumped slightly and glanced over her shoulder at him, almost as if she'd forgotten he was in the room. Very carefully, she rechecked the safety, reinserted the clip and replaced the gun on the table where she'd found it. "It's a good piece."

"You know your way around guns."

Her gaze remained on the Colt a moment longer. "It would seem so." She ran both hands down her thighs, as if to wipe away the feel of cold steel, a slight frown shadowing her face. It made him want to do something to erase the concern written there.

Instead, he picked up a clip and began loading it with cartridges. "Can you remember where you learned?" he asked. "Who taught you?"

"I wish to heaven I could," Mary answered softly, watching his quick, precise movements. "Are you expecting trouble?"

Jake recalled all that had happened in the short time since fate had thrust this woman into his life. "I always expect trouble," he said drily.

She raised her eyes to meet his. "I realize going back to that alley is risky," she said, her voice quiet, her words even. "And I know I'm asking a lot. But I don't have a choice. There might be some clue. Do you understand? I have to find out...."

Silently groaning, he set the clip aside. Did she have any idea what those clear green eyes of hers did to a man? Was she aware how persuasively they expressed her uncertainty, her vulnerability, conveyed her silent plea for help? Dammit, he didn't want to deal with this growing need to protect her that seemed to have come out of nowhere.

Caring for someone wasn't for him. He'd learned a long time ago to stay away from situations that he might become emotionally involved in. He'd never again allow himself to become a hostage to the future. He didn't make memories, didn't want them. Life had taught him they caused too much pain.

He sighed in resignation. "You're right. It won't be safe for either of us until we find out who you are," he said more to himself than to her. "Besides, without someone here to keep an eye on you, I figure you'd stay put for maybe five minutes after I leave."

Hope flared in her eyes, and she grinned. "Ten, tops."

Seeing her relax slightly gave him a great deal of satisfaction, and without thinking he reached out and brushed a finger across her slightly flushed cheek. Even as he savored the smooth warmth of her skin, his action astonished him. He had no reason to touch her, no reason at all. But he couldn't seem to stop himself. Nor did he remove his hand.

His touch was so unexpected that Mary trembled before she could control herself. For the briefest of seconds she thought she'd glimpsed sympathy—and a softening—in Jake's hard features. But that couldn't have been. There was no softness in this man, almost as if he believed to show it would prove fatal. For several heartbeats, she felt singed by the emotion barely hidden behind his sharp eyes.

Muttering an oath, Jake abruptly stepped back, severing the connection. He grabbed an empty clip as if to give his hands something less dangerous to do. "I want to make certain you understand what you're getting into," he said, his voice taking on a hard edge. "If someone recognizes you, things could get more than risky, real fast."

"That won't be a problem," she assured him, while trying to forget just how much this man could arouse her. "I'm good at disguises." She was coming to wonder if being around Jake put her at the greatest risk. The sooner she discovered who she was, the sooner she could get away from him.

"Yeah?" He raised an eyebrow. "How do you know?"

Confusion replaced the smile. Why did she believe she was good at disguises? A memory tugged at her. A memory of danger, of the need to protect her identity at all costs. That the consequence of being exposed would mean more than just danger to herself but to others, as well. But who? What? Frustration threatened to get the better of her. "I'm . . . not sure. It just feels right." Her smile returned, brighter this time because it was forced. "Give me a chance and we'll find out."

"All right," he said, studying her intently. "Let's see how good you are." He left the room to return shortly, carrying a leather jacket, a pair of women's running shoes and a baseball cap, the kind so popular with kids nowadays.

"This is the best I can do."

She reached for the cap first. In quick, economical movements she twisted her hair up into a knot, placed the cap over it and tucked the stray ends out of sight, then pulled the bill low over her face. Taking on a slouch and swagger that resembled Will's, she shoved her hands into the pockets of her sweats and sauntered across the room. "Well," she finally said when he didn't comment immediately, "what do you think?"

What he thought was that she was a natural-born actress. And he didn't much like the idea. "Except for the red toenails, you could pass for one of those punks Will runs with," he said, handing her the shoes.

"I'll take that as a compliment," she said drily and settled in a chair to put them on.

The shoes were too big. Her feet were small for such a tall woman. Small and sexy. Jake silently swore. He needed to steer clear of thoughts like those. "It would be interesting to see you in a decent pair of shoes."

"As long as I can walk in them, that's all that matters." She tested them out, finally stopping in front of Jake. Her expression grew serious. "I want to thank you for...everything."

"Better save that for when and if we make it back," he suggested, still hoping she might change her mind. The getup made her look younger, but it sure as hell didn't make her look any less sexy. It would be hard to conceal those curves, or a face that beautiful. Even free of makeup, she oozed sensuality. Hell, dressing like a boy just seemed to add to her sexiness, almost made her irresistible.

"It's getting dark." He grabbed his jacket and thrust it at her. "If you're determined to do this, we'd better get going."

Mary took the jacket from him and slid into it. It swallowed her, wrapping her in the comforting smell of well-worn leather. And Jake. This was Jake's coat...in Sondra's house. An unfamiliar emotion unfurled inside her. Did that mean there was something more than friendship between Sondra and Jake?

She turned to face him. "It must be convenient having a friend who keeps extra clothes—not to mention extra weapons—on hand for you," she commented, before she thought to stop herself.

"It goes much further than convenient," Jake told her cryptically, watching her upturned face. In his jacket she looked even more vulnerable—and sexy. His libido warred with a sudden need to ease the traces of anxiety still written there. The latter won. "Will is right, you know."

She looked startled. "About what?"

"Nothing we've learned about you proves anything."

His attempt to reassure her touched Mary in a way she was certain wasn't wise. "You put on a good show, McAlister, but you're not nearly as heartless as you'd like people to believe."

A muscle flexed in his jaw. "Don't take a statement of fact for anything except what it is," he warned. He picked up the gun and tucked it into the waistband of his jeans. "All I'm saying is that what evidence we've got is circumstantial."

"Circumstantial." She looked at him speculatively. "Isn't that a legal term? As I said before, you do talk like a cop. Or maybe an attorney."

This was the second time she'd alluded to his being a cop. If he wasn't careful, he was going to make a critical mistake. She was a damned sorceress, releasing inhibitions and weakening long-standing rules—something that years ago he'd learned never to allow. He needed to distract her, so he reached for the collar of her jacket on the pretext of straightening it. Smiling slightly, he said, "Damned few cops, let alone lawyers, would live in this part of town."

Her legs suddenly felt weak, and Mary knew beyond doubt that it had nothing whatsoever to do with the earlier blow to her head. Jake didn't release her collar. Instead, he continued to hold her immobile for long heartbeats, the intensity of his ice-blue gaze eclipsing everything else in the room. The world seemed to shrink until it encompassed only the two of them.

Jake took a step closer and breathed in the scent of her, an intoxicating mixture of something clean and unidentifiable. Her body was tantalizingly close. Too close. His fists tightened on the jacket as fire streaked straight to the lower region of his gut.

An answering heat coiled deep within Mary, and instinctively she swayed toward him.

Jake read the sensual awareness in her eyes and cursed. He'd succeeded in distracting her, all right, but in the process he'd unleashed a primal, potentially explosive element into the already highly charged situation. One he had serious doubts he could handle. He couldn't remember the last time he'd wanted a woman this fiercely. What made it worse was that he was all too conscious of the fact that she wanted him, too. Damn her, she wasn't even trying to hide her desire. And there wasn't one thing in hell he could do about it. Not when he didn't know who she was. Especially not when *she* didn't know who she was.

When, he wondered wryly, had he developed a noble streak?

He forced himself to release his grip on her and step back. It took considerably more effort than he would have liked. More than a little evidence suggested she could be a prostitute. Trouble was, he was beginning to suspect that even if he had proof positive, it wouldn't make one whit of difference to him.

"Let's get the hell out of here," he said gruffly, to keep himself from doing something stupid—like pulling her into his arms and finishing what his vivid imagination seemed intent on conjuring up.

The trip back to the alley seemed to take much less time than had the ride to Sondra's row house the night before. The late-evening shadows had deepened to the dark purple of a gathering storm, softening the details of the scene that sped past the car. But Mary recognized that they were getting close. She was grateful for the warmth of Jake's jacket. It not only warded off the October chill, but seemed to act as a talisman against her uneasy thoughts.

She wasn't certain she was ready to face what she might find once they reached their destination. Could she handle confirming she was a hooker? Of course, she reminded herself, that would be the least of her worries if this little expedition got one or both of them injured. Or worse.

She glanced over at Jake, and her stomach lurched with tension. She knew almost as much about this man as she did about herself—which at this point wasn't a whole heck of a lot. Yet trusting Jake McAlister was entirely too easy. Maybe it had something to do with his take-charge attitude—an attitude that said there was little he hadn't confronted and even less that he couldn't handle. Was she making a grave mistake? No point worrying at this late date, she reminded herself in resignation. She needed him. She had to get to the truth, and at the moment Jake was the only one she could turn to for help.

Rounding another corner, Jake stopped the car close to the same spot it had been parked the night before. An aeon ago. She felt his eyes on her for the first time since they'd left Sondra's.

"Ready?" he asked.

"As I'll ever be." But she made no move to open her door. Instead, she remained in her seat, groping for enough courage to get her through this with some dignity.

"Afraid?"

She was silent for a moment. "Yes," she admitted with candor. "But I'm more afraid of *not* knowing."

Thunder rumbled down the city streets, an ominous sound warning them away. Jake continued to study her. In a flash of lightning, he saw her fear, very stark, very real. It was something that up to this point she'd been careful to conceal. Seeing it clearly for the first time did strange things to him, things he wasn't prepared to deal with.

Jerking open his door, he got out of the car and came around to her side. He sent a quick glance up and down the street, making certain there were no curious bystanders, then opened her door and extended his hand.

Surprised, she accepted it. "I didn't think you were someone to observe social amenities," she said. His grip was firm and sure, and she gratefully absorbed the encouragement it conveyed.

"My sister taught me well," he told her.

She wanted to ask him to elaborate, but he didn't allow her the opportunity. He urged her quickly down the street, keeping close to the shadows.

It was completely dark by the time they reached their destination, the street deserted, the lone light bulb at the far end of the alley still giving scant illumination. She tugged against Jake's hold, and he seemed almost reluctant to let her go. She hesitated long enough to get her bearings, then walked over to the wooden crate still sprawled on its side.

The purse wasn't hard to find. It lay a few inches from the wall, its contents spread accusingly over the concrete. Condoms. Lots of them.

Ignoring the shiny leather bag, she picked up a handful of the small packets and let them slide through her fingers. Her every nerve ending was aware of Jake standing silently a few feet away, his gaze on her. After several ponderous seconds she looked up at him. ''I guess this kind of confirms it, huh?''

Chapter Six

Jake felt something fundamental inside him shift. Mary looked so stricken, and a part of him demanded that he wipe away the disillusionment dulling her brilliant green eyes. He had the strongest impulse to convince her that the evidence in front of them wasn't what it seemed. But he wasn't an impulsive man. In his line of work, being impulsive could get a man killed. All the same, the feeling didn't seem to want to go away. It was foreign, this need to comfort her. It made him feel . . . rusty.

"I can think of worse professions." It sounded lame, but it was the best he could come up with.

Her smile barely moved her lips, and even in the meager light he could see it hadn't reached her eyes. "A murderer, maybe?" she quipped.

The purr of an engine cut off any response on his part. A car was moving slowly down the deserted street toward them. It didn't necessarily mean danger, he told himself, trying to stem the flow of adrenaline pumping into his system, burning against his already raw nerves. He grabbed Mary and shoved her behind the crates, knocking her hat off in the process. As he had the night before, he shielded her body with his own. He wouldn't pull his gun unless given no other choice.

When the car came even with the alley, it paused. Mary instinctively pressed closer to Jake, the heavy beat of his heart not quite drowning out the engine's hum. As long seconds ticked by, his arm tightened around her, silently cautioning her to remain still.

Thunder boomed again, reverberating against the concrete and asphalt that held them trapped. As the first fat raindrops began to fall, the car edged away. Jake didn't release the breath he'd been holding until it had rounded the corner and disappeared from view.

"They've gone," he said, as he disentangled himself from her. He got to his feet and extended his hand.

She took it, shivering at the abrupt loss of his heat, and scrambled to her feet.

Jake felt the shudder move through her, and he had to rein in the desire to pull her to him again. *Stupid, McAlister.* He should have been thinking of getting them to safety, not offering her comfort.

"Let's get the hell back to the car before we get drenched." He grabbed Mary's hat and in his urgency barely gave her time to snatch up the very thing they'd come for—the purse.

They made it to the car just as the rain began in earnest. Once inside, Mary took a calming breath, holding the bag as if it were a ticking time bomb.

Fortunately Jake didn't give her a chance to debate whether to look inside it. He fired the engine and roared off into the enveloping darkness. After they'd gone several blocks, she realized they were headed away from Sondra's.

"Where are we going?"

"Nowhere in particular. I just wanted to drive for a while." Jake glanced at her, then back to the road. "Okay with you?"

She nodded, grateful for the postponement. For a short time she had an excuse to delay looking inside the purse she clutched in a death grip. Leaving danger behind, they rode in silence until Jake eventually pulled into a deserted roadside park overlooking the Potomac River and cut the engine.

The rain drummed on the roof, drowning out all other sound, closing the two of them into their own minuscule world. To gather her courage, Mary focused on the rain-distorted lights of Washington as they etched abstract designs in silver and ebony on the murky river water. After a few minutes, she reached overhead and turned on the interior light.

Heart thudding, she slowly opened the small shiny bag. Searching through its sparse contents didn't take long. If it had contained anything of value before, it was gone now. There was no wallet, no ID—only a tube of lipstick and a comb. And several more condoms.

"Nothing of value," she said, giving a shaky laugh. "Of course this day and age you'd think condoms would be worth a lot more than money."

She was agonizingly aware of Jake's steady gaze on her and the fact that he hadn't spoken. She couldn't bring herself to look at him. Finding no specific information about her, on top of the sight of more of those damned packets, was the ultimate blow. It closed off any option she might have had of escaping, or going to the police. How could she risk it now?

She'd fought it as long as she could, finally losing the struggle for composure. A lone tear escaped her careful control and slid down her cheek. "Who am I, Jake? Who the hell am I?"

Jake felt as if he'd been punched in the gut. Without considering the consequences, he reached for her and hauled her into his arms. She didn't hesitate but came willingly.

"I don't know," he said against her hair. "But we're going to find out." For such a tall woman, her body felt astonishingly delicate against him. She didn't make a sound, but he felt the slight shudders that racked her. They were the only indication that she was crying.

Minutes ticked by, but he continued to hold her. He didn't know much about giving comfort. He'd had little experience. Since Debbie's death, he'd closed off that part of himself. Instead he'd made it his mission to take down the people who took pleasure in causing pain and misery for others.

"Don't," he said after a time, surprised at how hoarse his voice sounded. "One of the best people I've ever known was a hooker."

She slowly raised her head to look at him. "That's hard to believe."

Her face was mere inches from his, tear streaked, her eyes puffy and red. In this condition she shouldn't be tempting. But she was.

She wiped at the tears with the back of her hand. It was a guileless, childlike gesture that made her seem fragile. And it tugged at him, maybe because something told him that she wasn't the type of woman who usually allowed anyone to see her this way.

Let go of her, a saner part of him prompted. But he didn't listen. He continued to hold her, watching as she regained her composure. She possessed an unusual inner strength, a strength he wondered if she fully appreciated.

Jake discovered that his initial desire to comfort was ripening into a desire for something much more basic. He would've thought that more or less confirming she was a prostitute would turn him off. It seemed to have no bearing on the beautiful woman in his arms. Right now he didn't give a damn who she was. Right now all he wanted was to taste her.

Mary read the intent in Jake's eyes. All she had to do was turn her head. But she didn't. She badly needed to connect with another human being. No, she amended, she needed to connect with this man—Jake McAlister—with his strength, with the security he represented.

When his mouth made the first searing contact with hers, she felt as if she'd been touched by a white-hot brand. She sensed the tightly checked tension in him, as if he'd been holding himself on a very short leash for a very long while. Liquid heat bubbled up from some secret place within her, and she felt as if she'd unlocked something she wasn't certain she could handle.

All the conflicting emotions Jake had felt for this woman, had tried to suppress, boiled over. Her mouth was soft and sweet and tasted exotic. And dangerous. He wasn't going to be able to get enough of her. Not here, not now. He was beginning to fear maybe not ever.

It was that last fragment of sane thought that forced him to break off the kiss and curse succinctly. Yeah, he reflected, very dangerous. If he pushed her, he warned himself, she might run. If he pushed himself, he might self-destruct.

It was the sudden sweep of lights illuminating the interior of the car as another vehicle pulled into the park that galvanized him into action. He set Mary away from him. Without a word, he started the car and drove off as if all the demons in hell were after him.

No doubt about it, this woman was a threat. A threat to his peace of mind and, worse, to his common sense. She called to his baser instincts. He couldn't believe he'd been stupid enough to park in a public place, even at this hour of the night, and start making out like some hormone-driven kid. Damned if he wasn't worse than Will.

What he needed to concentrate on was getting this woman out of his life as quickly as possible. What he *didn't* need to know was just how perfectly she fitted in his arms. Or the hot, sweet temptation of her mouth.

The rain had diminished to a slow drizzle, and Mary concentrated on the *thwack-thwack-thwack* of the windshield wipers. She didn't speak for several miles. She wasn't certain she could say anything coherent. The imprint of Jake's mouth remained vivid in her memory, as if he'd just released hers. She touched a finger to her lips. They were swollen and tender, as if they'd been sensitized to Jake Mc-

Alister. The lower region of her abdomen still burned with the liquid heat of arousal. Had she ever been kissed like that? Had she ever responded to another man in that same mind-melting manner? Somehow she doubted it. It would be impossible to forget something with the power to shake her to the soles of her feet.

Covertly, she studied Jake. He drove as he did everything else in her short experience with him—with careless efficiency, his expression unreadable. He gave no indication that he was experiencing any of the emotional upheaval that racked her. The dashboard's dim light threw his harsh features into relief, emphasizing the dangerous quality that seemed a basic part of him. Now she had one more reason to fear him.

"Talk to me, Jake," she finally said, to break the silence that had become uncomfortable. She was grateful her voice sounded normal.

He sent her a brief glance, then refocused his attention on the road stretching out ahead of them. "What do you want me to tell you?"

As always, he seemed in perfect control, as if nothing unusual had transpired between them. She fingered the useless purse lying where she'd abandoned it on the seat beside her.

"Anything," she said. "Since we can't talk about me, tell me something about you."

His expression became wary. "Like what?"

"Tell me about this woman you think's so great, even though you say she's a...hooker." Against her will, Mary identified the emotion unfolding inside her. Jealousy. Jealousy of a nameless, faceless woman who might be a prostitute but who obviously meant something to Jake. "Who is she?"

"Was," Jake corrected, saying the word without inflection. "She was my sister. And she's dead."

Unprepared for his stark honesty, Mary sucked in a sharp breath. She'd expected him to tell her about some long-ago lover. Or maybe one not so long ago. She hadn't expected this. "I'm sorry. That was thoughtless of me. I didn't intend to open old wounds. I just wanted to take my mind off my own troubles."

"No," he said after a brief silence. "I think I'd like to talk about her."

Surprise warred with unreasonable pleasure that he was willing to share something this personal with her. Mary tucked one leg under her, turned on the seat so that she could watch his face and waited.

"Debbie practically raised me," he began. "She was eight years older than me, but she hadn't had a chance to do much with her life when our mother died. Debbie'd always had big dreams. She could've stuck me in foster care or some orphanage. But she didn't. Instead she gave up her dreams and took over looking after a snot-nosed kid who was more trouble than he was worth."

His comment had been delivered carelessly, but her heart squeezed painfully at the underlying self-reproach. "I'm sure your sister felt you were worth it."

Jake's gaze sliced to hers, and she saw the rawness that darkened his eyes. "Maybe. I certainly didn't deserve it."

"You shouldn't talk that way about yourself."

He shrugged. "Why? I've never believed in lying to myself. When she needed me, I was useless."

Oddly, it angered her that he could deprecate himself in this manner, and she chose to change the subject slightly. "Where did you grow up?"

"The projects."

"In D.C.?"

"Close enough."

"What was it like, where you lived?" At that particular moment, she couldn't say whether she was pursuing this in hopes of learning more about Jake or gaining some glimmer of recognition about her own life.

Jake took the ramp onto the Washington Beltway and headed north. "I wouldn't call it living. More like survival of the fittest."

"You make it sound like a war zone."

There was an edge to his laugh. "The description doesn't do it justice. At least in a war zone you can identify your enemies. Where I'm from, it's a calculated guess at best. And if you guess wrong, you can get killed."

Mary turned that around in her mind for several seconds. During her short time with Jake, several things had stirred hazy memories. But there was nothing familiar about what he was telling her now. Had she grown up in similar surroundings? "Then why didn't you move?"

"No place else to go. At least we knew people there, knew where to go to get what we needed just to stay alive."

"Didn't you have a relative who'd take you in?"

"None that we knew about. Certainly none that claimed us."

She had little trouble imagining what that must have been like. It was too close to how she felt at the moment. "What about an agency?"

Jake snorted derisively. "Debbie knew the chances were better than even that we'd be separated if an agency got its hands on us."

She hugged herself to ward off the sudden chill. "So how did you live?"

"Debbie took odd jobs." She watched his face, illuminated by the headlights of oncoming traffic, soften. "I used to think it was great when she worked as a waitress."

Intrigued, she asked, "What made that special?"

"Extra food," he said simply. "She'd bring home leftovers. If I really got lucky, she'd bring home some gooey dessert." He shook his head and grinned. "Probably worse than eating nothing at all, but it sure tasted good."

Jake, the man, was so self-contained, so utterly in control, that it was hard for Mary to imagine a much younger version eagerly awaiting such a simple treat. Her heart turned over at the idea. "How old was Debbie when your mother died?"

"Sixteen. Old enough to drop out of school. Old enough to get a job."

Sixteen. Much too young to be worrying about raising a child. She should have been thinking about what she was going to do with her life or about boys or about what she was going to wear to the next prom.

A memory flickered, a snippet of floating down a curving staircase in an expensive white gown. But it wasn't a pleasant memory, though objectively Mary realized it ought to have been. She tried to focus the scene, but it stayed obscured by the mist surrounding her thoughts.

"That would have made you somewhere around eight or nine. Right?" Maybe if she kept him talking, the memory would become clearer, more detailed.

"Yeah. Too young to be much help. Old enough to find trouble."

Mary couldn't contain a chuckle. "Now why don't I have a problem imagining that? Was your sister strict?"

A corner of Jake's mouth lifted, but the smile was sad. "I could run her ragged at times, but she mostly tolerated it." His fingers flexed around the steering wheel. "There was only one rule she wouldn't bend on. No drugs."

"And you stuck to that one."

He searched her eyes for a moment before turning his attention back to the road. "Don't be too certain. It can get you in trouble."

An enigmatic warning from an enigmatic man. Nonetheless Mary was as sure as if he'd given the answer under oath.

"If you grow up around drugs, see what they can do to friends, to the community, to someone you love—" He stopped abruptly. "No, I didn't break it. But she did."

He delivered the statement in a voice that was almost unemotional. Almost. She felt a hole open up in the region of her heart. "Oh, my God," she whispered. "Why?"

He didn't answer immediately, and Mary became aware that they were headed back toward his part of D.C. "Debbie dreamed of getting out, both of us starting a new life somewhere else. She heard about a program being offered in the neighborhood to teach office skills to...disadvantaged women, and she signed up."

"Sounds like a smart move," Mary said.

"Depends."

"On...?"

The muscle at his jaw tensed. "Whether the people running the show are really interested in helping or whether they're in it for themselves."

"I don't think I understand," she said. "Who was running it?"

"A bunch of do-gooders who couldn't find any better way to spend their free time. Figured they'd run down here a few hours a week, ease their consciences by solving the problems of people less...fortunate. They were *outsiders*, dammit." The word was an epithet.

In the dim light his expression was grim. "They were meddling in something they couldn't possibly understand. They didn't give a damn about what someone like Debbie needed.

"They promised she'd make enough money to get herself and me out of the slums. So she bought in to their promises. Everyone liked Debbie," he said, his voice softening again. "She was beautiful and talented. But too damned trusting."

Mary narrowed her eyes in confusion. "Was that wrong?"

Jake cut her a look that said nobody could be that naive. "One of the volunteers, a woman named Barbara, became great pals with her. Barbara was a society type." He made it sound, Mary noted, like an insult.

"Society type," she repeated thoughtfully. "How exactly would you define that?"

"Someone who doesn't know what it's like to go to bed hungry or wonder where her next decent clothes will come from. Someone who doesn't have to worry whether the landlord will wait one more day for his rent before he kicks you out of your fine roach-and-rat-infested palace. Someone who feels guilty because she's had all the advantages of life handed to her. So she decides to absolve the guilt by sticking her nose in where it doesn't belong."

"And that describes Barbara?"

He laughed, but the sound was hollow. "She considered helping out 'less fortunate people' her current social obligation. She was also into modeling, and that fascinated Debbie."

Mary frowned. An image of being dressed in a skimpy bathing suit, poised under blinding photography lights raced through her mind. *"That's it, darlin',"* a voice purred, while a camera clicked and whirled. *"Let me see that beautiful smile. Give me all you've got."*

Even in memory she didn't like the voice. Shaken, she forced herself to concentrate on Jake. His white-knuckled grip on the steering wheel and his tension brought her thoughts back to what he was telling her.

"Barbara made Debbie her latest pet project," he continued. "Got her interested in modeling. Debbie certainly had the looks for it. Found her a job. Introduced her to her country-club set. To someone from Debbie's background, it seemed like a fairy tale."

Mary experienced another sliver of recognition.

"But Debbie couldn't handle it. Life in the fast lane was too tempting. And she broke her number-one rule. She started messing with drugs."

Her breath caught in her chest. "But why?" Mary asked, trying to comprehend what could've pushed his sister to jeopardize her chances of success in this particular manner.

"Everyone else was doing it." He grimaced. "How many times have you heard that? More than anything, Debbie wanted to belong. When Barbara discovered Debbie's little problem, she told her to get lost. That left Debbie with an expensive habit and no way to support it." He shifted restlessly in his seat. "There wasn't a damned thing I could do to stop her. Or help her."

"Oh, Jake. What could you have done? How old were you?" She ached for the boy who'd had to stand by and watch this happen, to endure this tragedy alone, who'd believed he carried the heavy burden of protecting an older sister all by himself.

"Twelve, maybe thirteen. But my age doesn't excuse me." His eyes cut to her, and in the dim light she read the anguish in them. "She found the quickest way to raise the most money."

"How?" she pressed, not wanting to know, but somehow knowing he needed to finish it.

"She sold herself."

There was such anger and pain in those words, such a sense of betrayal. Had *she* done this to someone who'd loved her? Having witnessed what it had done to Jake, Mary didn't think she could live with the knowledge if she had. "I truly am sorry."

"Yeah," he said, his voice stripped of emotion, "so am I."

"Why are you still here, then? Why didn't you get out just as soon as you were old enough?"

"Simple," he said. "My business is here."

Jake flicked a quick glance at Mary, sitting so quietly beside him on the front seat. She hadn't spoken for several miles. He'd be glad when they reached Sondra's. Anything that broke the silence stretching between them would be a welcome relief.

Damn! What in hell had come over him? He'd told this woman things he'd never told another living soul. Not even Sondra, certainly never a stranger. She was the first woman in a very long time, he realized, who'd been able to make him forget his hard-held rules. Not once, he reflected in disgust, but twice.

The kiss had been bad enough, but he could excuse himself for that slip. After all, she was beautiful—not to mention sexy as sin. Against his will his body responded to the mental image, and he silently groaned. He had the same urges as any healthy male, and there hadn't been time for a woman in his life in longer than he cared to remember.

But spilling his guts to her had been plain stupid. He was aware of the dangers. A man never knew who his enemy might be. He'd learned that the hard way.

He understood how she'd gotten to him. Her desperate request for conversation, a request that had been more a plea—one he couldn't bring himself to refuse. She'd needed a distraction, and the haunted look in her eyes had coerced him into providing it. Then he'd discovered there was something liberating—almost seductive—about talking to someone with no memory.

Or had it been the fact it was Mary he'd been talking to? She'd listened as if she was really interested in what he had to say. But it was more than that. She'd known just how to ask the right questions, just how to lure him into revealing one more bit of information about himself. And she'd known when to remain silent. Talking to her hadn't felt like talking to a stranger. It had felt...comfortable. Disturbingly so.

Hell, yes, she was good. She was a pro. And it was getting remarkably difficult to keep his guard up around her.

Mary waited until they'd reached the safety of Sondra's house before breaking the silence. Standing just inside the front door, she turned to Jake. He seemed much too close. "I appreciate what you did for me tonight." She attempted a smile, but it was tinged with disappointment. "Although it seems to have been a waste of time."

"Not a waste," he said, holding his voice steady. "Even the smallest piece of information can be useful."

"I did have a couple of flashes of memory, but not enough to make much sense. That's what makes it so disheartening. It's so close, just out of reach." She made a frustrated sound.

"Give it time." Why wasn't he encouraging her— better yet, helping her—to probe whatever she'd remembered, to examine it for any added shred of information? But even as he admitted that the situation was keeping him from getting the Brady case back on track, he couldn't bring himself to push Mary. She'd been through enough in the last 24-plus hours. He didn't want to add to it. Even though good sense told him to keep his hands to himself he reached out and tucked a strand of hair behind her ear. It felt silky warm to his fingers, and he had to restrain himself from plunging his hands into the honey-gold mass.

Her gaze darted to his as if she'd read his thoughts. He couldn't remember ever having seen eyes quite her shade of clear green. They seemed to reach a part of him he'd learned to keep hidden. A stare as direct as hers, seeming without guile, could lull him into believing she couldn't have been a hooker, no matter what the evidence. If he let it.

With effort he stepped back and sent her a crooked smile. "It's only been a couple of days. What's the rush? I'm beginning to think you don't like my company."

She looked startled before giving him a thousand-watt smile that didn't quite reach her eyes. "Now how could I not like the company of such a charming host?"

He chuckled, but a warning siren went off in his brain. He'd seen smiles like that hundreds of times as he'd walked the streets. It was part of the stock-in-trade. Hookers had never interested him in the past. It wasn't that he had anything against them. He had a policy—he left them alone and they left him alone.

There'd only been one he'd cared anything about—and that had been for the simple reason she'd been his sister. Trouble was, the feelings this woman stirred in him were about as far from brotherly as they could get. If he were honest with himself, he'd admit he was relieved the trip back to the alley hadn't been very useful. Fact was, he was discovering he wasn't all that eager to have Mary disappear from his life.

This much honesty, he decided grimly, could give a man nightmares.

"Time for bed, Helen of Troy. You can take Sondra's bed."

She looked at him, weariness etching her features. "But where will you sleep?"

"Are you offering to share?" Jake watched her weariness change to confusion and that pleased him. At least it put them on an equal footing. It also raised a question. Why would a prostitute, even one with amnesia, be thrown by a proposition—particularly one made in jest?

She recovered quickly. "No. I'm offering you the whole thing."

"Now, that," he said, running his eyes wickedly down the length of her, "isn't much of an enticement. Thanks, but I'll find a place to bunk down. Get some rest. We'll tackle this again tomorrow."

He thought she was going to argue—he almost hoped she would. Maybe an all-out fight would clear the air. At the very least it would help burn off some of the excess energy pumping through him. But he wasn't going to be that lucky. After a moment's deliberation, she relented. "Perhaps that's best. Good night, then."

"Right," Jake said, watching her climb the stairs to the second floor. Through the thin walls separating them, Jake could hear her moving around in the small bedroom. He hoped she got some rest. He sure as hell knew he wasn't going to.

Chapter Seven

As Mary exited the bathroom the next morning, the sound of Jake and Will engaged in a heated discussion stopped her. Ignoring a twinge of guilt, she moved carefully down the stairs to the kitchen door with every intention of eavesdropping.

She'd decided, during the long sleepless hours before dawn, that it was in her best interests to get away from this man who roused such primitive responses in her—responses, she recognized on some elemental feminine level, that were unique to Jake McAlister. And all the more dangerous because of it. Maybe this was her opportunity.

"You can't tell me what to do! You're not my father!" Will yelled. Mary wondered if the underlying hurt was as plain to Jake as it was to her. "You don't own me. You're nothing to me, man."

Jake's anger was equally clear though quieter. "Right on all counts."

"So..." Will said, his level of intensity subsiding somewhat, "why're you trying?"

"Maybe because I've been there. Maybe because I don't want to see you make stupid mistakes."

"Aw, man, don't give me that crap. You don't even understand."

"Don't I?"

"Hell, no," Will shot back. "Adults never do."

"Maybe. But that doesn't change the fact," Jake stated in measured words, "that you are to stay away from those punks."

On that ultimatum, he stalked out of the kitchen, nearly colliding with Mary. He didn't break stride as he brushed past and headed for the front door. "Keep an eye on him," he flung over his shoulder at her. "I need some air."

Mary deliberated with the idea of waiting until it was safe, then leaving by the same route. But she couldn't bring herself to desert Will. Not simply because Jake had asked—or was that ordered?—her to keep an eye on him but because the kid sounded as if he could use a friend right about now. With misgiving, she entered the kitchen.

Will sat straddling a chair with his arms resting across the back. He glanced at Mary and let out a frustrated sigh. "He doesn't understand," he repeated.

"You want to talk about it?" Great, she thought. Her first opportunity to get away, and instead she was offering to discuss Will's problems with him—when any idiot knew nobody could talk sense to a teenager. Of course, she reminded herself, Will wasn't the average teenager.

"Aw, Jake has it in for my friends. I guess I could live with that," he added on an angry edge, "if he didn't include Cilla."

Mary went to the refrigerator and opened it. "Want some breakfast?"

"No... thanks. Any sodas left?"

She mentally shrugged. Why not? She took out the last two cans, placed one in front of Will and took the chair opposite him.

"Who's Cilla?"

He snagged his soda and popped it open. "A friend."

"As in girlfriend?"

Color washed up in his cheeks. "Kinda."

He was a tall kid, built like a basketball player, all knobby knees and sharp elbows but exhibiting the first promise of masculine strength. And beauty. His unique blend of heritages showed in his slightly slanted hazel eyes, high cheekbones and olive complexion.

She could imagine Jake at Will's age with the same masculine appeal. And like Jake, she reflected, trying to suppress the memory of last night's mind-blowing kiss, Will was going to be a heartbreaker. If he wasn't already.

Despite all his belligerence, she liked the kid. And she could understand why Jake was concerned about him.

"And Jake doesn't approve of her? Is that what all the shouting's about?"

"Aw, he's always yelling at me."

"Maybe because he cares?" she ventured.

Will made a rude comment. "He don't approve of nothing I do."

"Could be he *does* understand," she offered, wondering why she persisted in trying to convince Will that Jake wasn't the ogre he thought. How the heck did she know? But somehow she did.

"Jake won't give Cilla a break," he said, glowering at her. "She's cool. She's just hanging with the wrong crowd."

Mary opened her can of soda, then took a sip. "Are you involved with this crowd?"

He shifted uneasily. "I gotta, y'know? So I can keep an eye on her."

"Ah, I see. And why is it necessary for you to keep an eye on her?"

"Cilla's a really hot babe, and the guys...well, they really dig her."

"You really like this girl, huh?"

Though he tried to cover it with nonchalance, embarrassment heated his face. "Yeah. But I can't figure out what she likes in a guy."

"Well, for one thing, I can guarantee she *doesn't* like to be called a 'really hot babe.'"

"You don't think so?" He mulled that over for a minute or two. "Then what does she like? You're a babe—I mean...you know..." He looked at her with eyes serious beyond his years. "Can you tell me what to do?"

"You want me to give it to you straight?" she asked. "Or do you want me to take your side against Jake?"

His hazel eyes turned wary. "That means I'm not gonna like what you're gonna say, right?"

She grinned. "Probably."

He huffed out a breath. "Tell me straight, I guess."

"Good answer." She had the urge to reach over and tousle his short-cropped hair, which was a ludicrous notion, considering he was taller than she, not to mention the fact that he'd probably take it as an insult. "Most important thing you can do is show her respect."

"Ah, jeez, I knew it," he groused. "You sound just like Jake."

"Uh-oh." It was a struggle, but Mary maintained a straight face. "I guess that's bad."

Will sighed and the fight seemed to go out of him. "Nah...not bad." He lifted his shoulders and let them fall back into place. "It's just that he doesn't know what it's like."

For all Will's animosity toward Jake, Mary again sensed the bond between them. And Will's desire to please the man.

"Oh, I don't know. You might be underestimating him," she suggested, visualizing the dark, enigmatic man who had a knack for handling trouble. "Does he have something to be concerned about?"

"Whaddaya mean?"

"Are these guys into things they shouldn't be?"

She watched him take a swig from his soda, recognizing a delaying tactic when she saw one. "Maybe." It was as truthful an answer as most teenagers would give when pressed to snitch on a friend.

"So, are you going to elaborate or do I use my imagination?"

"He—heck no, don't do that," he said emphatically. "You guys always exaggerate everything." He shrugged. "Maybe some of the dudes are messing around with, y'know, stuff."

"Ah."

"But not all of them," he hastened to add.

"Stuff" could run the gamut from drugs to gangs, she realized, suppressing a shiver. "Just what exactly are we talking about here?"

He sent her another wary look but didn't answer.

"Okay, you don't like that question," she commented thoughtfully. "Let's try this one. Which group do you fit in? The ones who do... or the ones who don't?"

"I'm not crazy," he said quietly, as a flash of maturity slipped past his sullen facade. "I know to stay away from that junk."

"Smart." She was amazed and disturbed by the relief his straight answer gave her. Getting personally involved in Will's life, she silently warned, was not a good idea. She had enough problems of her own. But the warning didn't seem to take. "What about Cilla— is she as smart?"

A worried expression pinched his features. "She's cool. For now."

Mary contemplated how to proceed. Will was asking for guidance, and she wondered fleetingly if a prostitute was qualified to give it. "You tell Cilla for me that if she wants to hang on to her looks, she better stay away from drugs." She took another sip of her drink. "If she's half as smart as she's pretty, she'll want you to stay away from them, too."

He looked doubtful. "All the really cool guys do it."

She shook her head. "Only the stupid ones."

"Yeah, that's what Jake says."

"Perhaps you should listen?"

"Why?" he asked, slipping back into his belligerent-teenager role.

"Because I think he cares a great deal about what happens to you," Mary told him again. "Why else would he be on your case?"

Will made a scoffing sound. "Jake doesn't need nobody. I could disappear and he'd never notice."

"I think you're wrong," she said softly, a part of her cautioning that she was overstepping her bounds and meddling where she had no right. Again she ignored the warning. "I think he needs you."

A flare of hope momentarily replaced the disbelief on his face, but then he shook his head in denial.

"Well, do me a favor and don't disappear just yet," she said. "You may think he doesn't need you, but *I* do."

He looked skeptical. "You don't need me. You got Jake."

"Ah." She raised an eyebrow in mock puzzlement. "Then you do think there're some advantages to having him around?"

"Maybe." The concession was made grudgingly. "Jake knows how to take care of business."

A chill passed over her. Jake had said something about business just last night. *"My business is here,"* he'd told her and made it sound ominous. Meaning what? What kind of business? And why couldn't she get him to talk about it? The secrets she sensed surrounding Jake raised her suspicions and made her uneasy.

Why did she keep getting hints of something forbidden and not quite licit concerning him? But it didn't make sense. After what he'd told her the other night, it didn't seem possible he could be into drugs.

But if he were, why would he care if Will got involved with them? In some corner of her mind, she
was aware that drug dealers seldom messed with their
own poison. Her head began to ache. It was all too
confusing. Nothing about Jake McAlister made
sense.

"Well, right now I can use all the help I can get,"
she said.

"What kind of help do you need?"

"I don't know who I am," she said, giving him a
level look, "or where I belong. And I very badly need
to find out."

For several seconds Will seemed to weigh the va-
lidity of her statement, then accept it as truth. "So
that's why Jake's been asking all those questions," he
said. "That might be cool, not to remember anything, y'know?"

His reaction surprised her since it was so similar to
Jake's. "You think so?"

"Yeah. You wouldn't have to think about being
lonely. You could forget all the bad stuff."

He sounded wistful and philosophical all at the
same time. Appalled, she asked, "Is there a lot of bad
stuff in your life?"

He shifted uncomfortably. "I guess it depends on
what you think's bad. What's it like, not knowing
who you are?"

She rubbed her arms absently. "Scary, mostly. But
it's...lonely, too. It's like you have nobody in the
world who cares about you."

A frown came and went on his face. "That's
rough," he said seriously. "A lot of folks around here
know about being lonely and scared. That's why
gangs have so much power." He suddenly stopped, as

if realizing he'd said too much. "Well . . . some guys think so." He got up and threw his empty can into the garbage.

Something was going on here, something she knew intuitively she couldn't let drop. "Gangs? How do they help?"

Will prowled the small room like a trapped animal. "A gang's like family, y'know? There's a lot of kids who don't have nobody, and the gang takes care of 'em. But once they get hold of you, they'll never let you go. The only way out is if you're dead."

Mary felt the cold rush of fear and had to clear her throat twice to keep it from her voice. "Do you buy that?"

He stared at her with eyes that had seen far more than anyone should ever see in a lifetime, much less sixteen short years. "Nobody tells me what to do," he told her flatly.

This time she didn't question the surge of relief flooding her. But his reasoning didn't really surprise her. He was too independent to be part of a gang. Just like Jake, she realized with a pang, Will had already become a loner, already learned how to close himself off from those around him. Except for Cilla. And Jake.

Who did Jake have?

"So what's troubling you?" she asked softly, trying to still the ache in her chest.

"It's Cilla," he said, his face pinched with worry. "The dudes she's messing with are bad news." He took a deep breath. "So, no matter what Jake says, I gotta watch out for her, y'know?"

"Have you told Jake what you've told me?"

Will shook his head. "He won't listen. He just yells and walks out."

Young though Will was, she knew no orders or demands or lectures were going to work in this situation with this man-child. All she could do was try persuasion and caution. "It wouldn't be smart to make the same mistakes you're trying to keep Cilla from making. And it might be wise to cut Jake a little slack."

His shrug effectively told her Will wasn't ready to discuss it. "Don't worry about anything," he said, changing subjects. "If Jake won't help you, I will."

She found his concern for her sweetly touching. Again she had to be impressed with his maturity. A lump lodged in her throat, and she had to swallow before she could speak.

"Thanks, Will. I really appreciate it." This time she didn't resist the urge to reach over and squeeze his arm. Surprisingly, he didn't pull away; in fact, he didn't seem to mind.

A slight movement out in the hall caught her attention, and she looked up to find Jake filling the doorway. Except for the intent look on his face, he gave no hint of how much he'd heard or what he was thinking.

"Is this conversation open to anyone, or should I come back later?" But he strolled into the room and over to the refrigerator without waiting for a reply. After determining that there were no more sodas inside, he pulled out the chair next to Mary and straddled it.

He was close enough to trigger a flutter of sensual awareness deep inside her. He smelled of soap and freshly laundered clothes. He must have showered recently, and she wondered fleeting where, since she hadn't heard water running. Gone was the bandanna, his dark hair slicked back, held in place by the lingering dampness. Despite the cool weather, he'd exchanged his usual jeans, vest and T-shirt for a pair of shorts and a tank shirt. They revealed muscled arms and shoulders obviously well acquainted with hard physical labor.

Mary scrambled to collect herself. "By all means," she said, hoping she sounded blasé, "join us."

One side of Jake's mouth quirked. He picked up her half-finished soda and held it up. "Do you mind?" Without waiting for permission, he took a drink.

Watching Jake put his mouth where hers had been only moments ago was intimate and somehow shocking. She was certain what he was doing was perfectly innocent. He was thirsty and she was simply supplying the means to quench his thirst. With each swallow, the muscles in his throat worked in a slow up-and-down slide. She felt another odd little quiver, as if he were drinking from her instead of the metal can. She dragged her eyes away, afraid of what he might read there.

He emptied the can and set it down. The hollow click of metal against the tabletop jerked her gaze back to his face.

"Anyone up for a game of basketball?" he asked casually.

The gloomy expression lifted from Will's features. "You're on, man," he said without hesitation, their recent disagreement apparently forgotten. "Just tell me when and where."

Jake turned his gaze on her. "What about you? You want to come watch?"

"Watch, hell," Mary said with feeling. "I want to play." Right this minute the thought of anything physical had enormous appeal to her. She'd been cooped up for three days with only adrenaline—and Jake McAlister—for stimulation. Yes, she definitely needed exercise, the more rigorous the better.

Surprise flitted over Jake's features. "Are you sure your head can stand the strain?"

"Don't worry about my head. It's just fine." She paused then, to still the tiny, persistent voice that whispered caution, and asked, "Is it safe?"

He continued to look at her intently. "Have I failed you so far?"

Another question for a question, thrown out lightly but containing something deeper, something she didn't want to examine too closely. She cocked her head. "Well…it could be a trap," she said, trying for a teasing note, "since I'm not sure I've ever played before."

He waited a beat, then gave Will a decidedly conspiratorial wink. "That's okay," Jake said magnanimously. "We'll be glad to give you pointers. Right, Will?"

"Yeah," Will agreed and grinned. "Just follow our lead, and don't worry about a thing."

"I'll try not to disappoint you," she said drolly.

After rounding up a pair of Sondra's shorts and a sleeveless shirt for her to wear under her sweats, Jake and Will took Mary to a neighborhood located a safe distance from the house. It was in an area that had begun to show the first burgeoning signs of renewed pride. Here and there a house displayed evidence of recent repairs or a new coat of paint, a yard cleared of rubbish and freshly planted with shrubbery. Unlike so many others she'd been exposed to in the past several days, this neighborhood had an upbeat feel to it, as if a measure of hope had been restored along with the improvements.

The basketball court was located in an ancient warehouse, its floors scuffed and worn from years of use, its nets frayed around the edges. But it served the purpose she wanted—which was to work up a sweat. And it felt fabulous.

Getting into the spirit of the game certainly hadn't taken Mary long, Jake noted with amusement, as he wiped his forehead with the back of his arm. She threw herself into it with the obvious objective of winning. And she was no slouch, either, he conceded, still smarting from the thorough trouncing she'd delivered to him and Will two out of three games. He shook his head wryly. They'd been hustled. She must have played basketball before.

He studied her as she dribbled down the court, maneuvering for her next lay-up. Her face flushed with victory, she was totally unselfconscious, clearly exhilarating in what she was doing. Wet strands of hair escaped the haphazard ponytail she'd pulled it into. Perspiration glistened on her well-toned shoulders and soaked through her thin cotton shirt.

The damp fabric hinted at nicely shaped breasts. Jake silently groaned. The urge to run his tongue over her skin to discover if she tasted as delicious as she looked was almost overpowering. Would she make love with the same abandon? The thought came out of nowhere, and his body instantly tightened in response. He muttered a curse. Considering the brevity of what he was wearing, he'd do well to keep his mind above the waist.

"Jake!" Will shrieked, as Mary worked her way into position. "Watch what you're doing, man, or she's going to beat us again!"

He forced his attention back to the game. "I'm on her," he assured Will. *Yeah, right.*

Mary laughed a bet-you-can't-stop-me laugh, the sound echoing off the cavernous walls. She'd just started to take her shot when the double doors at the far end of the makeshift gym burst open, and a man, with the size and build of a professional boxer, slammed into the room.

Mary halted in midthrow. The ball dropped from her hands and rolled across the floor to stop at the feet of the hulking intruder. He reached down, scooped it up in one giant hand and hefted it a couple of times.

"Well, what have we here?" boomed a deep, gravelly voice that perfectly complemented the newcomer's appearance.

Jake watched Mary surreptitiously move closer to Will, placing herself in the correct defensive posture to protect him. Her automatic reaction to protect someone who was little more than a stranger touched a part of Jake he'd guarded for years. And made him angry.

Crazy woman. Didn't she even consider the possibility that she might be putting her life in danger? Besides it was ludicrous, considering Will was already taller than she and probably knew a hell of a lot more about protecting himself than she would ever learn. But she was good, he'd give her that. In a tight situation, he'd be damned grateful to have someone with her instincts at his back. Still, a part of him questioned where and how she'd acquired them.

Jake moved up beside her, casually placing a hand on her arm. Her muscles felt taut under his fingers, as if she was ready to spring into action. "Try not to pass out on me again."

He spoke in a low voice close to her ear. This wasn't the first time he'd said that to her. Mary didn't know whether to be relieved or angered by the suggestion of humor lurking in Jake's softly spoken command. Either way she allowed herself to relax slightly, while keeping her senses on full alert.

"Careful, Nathan," Jake said mildly, gently ushering her toward the new arrival. "I think you're scaring our visitor." As he spoke, a smile was already transforming the other man's face.

"Jake, you old son of a gun." He threw the ball to Will's waiting hands. "And Will. It's about time you showed up again."

Will gave the ball a couple of bounces and mumbled a greeting, then headed for the hoop at the far end of the court.

"We stopped by to shoot a few hoops," Jake said. "Figured you wouldn't mind."

"You know you're welcome anytime, Jake. I heard the ruckus and came to see who was causing it," the other man said.

Jake pushed Mary forward slightly. "Mary, this is Nathan Garner. Nathan, meet Mary. He's the minister who runs things around this dilapidated excuse for a church."

Minister? Mary ran a quick eye up and down him. He was dressed more like someone off the streets than a clergyman, and from the looks of him, he could move small mountains single-handedly. "Reverend Garner," she said, trying to keep the incredulity from her voice.

His eyes warmed, but she caught a hint of profound sadness in them. "We don't stand on formality around here, Mary," he said, extending his hand, "so please, just call me Nathan. Welcome to my corner of the world. "

"It's a pleasure to meet you . . . Nathan." She returned his handshake, then sent Jake an accusing glance. "Jake failed to mention the basketball court was located in a church. Now I understand why he said it was safe."

"Well, it's safer than it was, but we've got a ways to go." He turned to Jake, a teasing note entering his voice. "So where did you two meet up?"

Mary started to speak, but Jake tightened his hold on her arm, signaling silence. "It's a long story."

Nathan sobered. "I'm good with long stories. And problems," he added almost as an afterthought.

An indefinable look passed between the two men. "Thanks," Jake said. "Maybe later."

"All right, then," Nathan said, seeming to accept the topic as closed. "Since at the moment I can't help you, perhaps you'd be willing to give me a hand."

Jake's eyes narrowed. "Just how big a hand are we talking about here?"

"Now, Jake." The minister's tone took on a coaxing quality, the suggestion of mischief in his eyes barely concealed. "It's just a small project."

"Small? If I remember correctly, the last time you had me help with a 'small' project, I had trouble moving for the better part of the next week."

"Nothing that difficult this time," he assured Jake good-naturedly. "I just want a few stones laid for a walkway in the rectory garden."

Jake released a deep sigh and looked at Mary. "This may or may not," he muttered sardonically, "take a while. Okay with you?"

She spread her hands. "I have nowhere else pressing to go. Is there anything I can do?"

"Careful," he warned. "Once Nathan discovers a willing worker, he takes it as an open-ended commitment to be at his beck and call."

"Now don't go making me out to be a harsh taskmaster," Nathan scolded in his deep voice. "I just met Mary. I wouldn't dream of imposing on her."

"Uh-huh. Don't let him fool you," Jake told Mary. "It's that innocent act that'll lure you in every time."

Nathan's expression became sheepish, and Mary couldn't help laughing. She had no doubt the man was a master at getting his way. "That's all right. I'll take my chances," she told them.

"Bless you, my child," he said, trying to sound suitably offended, and Jake rolled his eyes heavenward.

Leaving Will still shooting hoops, Nathan led Jake and Mary to a small office with a doorway opening into a private garden. It didn't take him long to show them what he wanted done. Then he excused himself, leaving the two of them alone. Traffic noises from the nearby street filtered into the room, a reminder that the real world wasn't far away.

Mary suddenly felt awkward. Her cotton shirt, damp with perspiration, clung stickily to her skin. She picked up a corner of the material to wipe her face.

Jake pulled a towel from a duffel bag she hadn't noticed he'd brought with him and held it out to her.

She took it from his outstretched hand. "Thanks," she said, her smile off-center. She wiped her face and pulled on her sweats. "You always seem to be prepared."

He studied her for several heartbeats. "Not always," he said. "I wasn't prepared for you."

Without looking back, he opened the door and walked out into the garden.

Chapter Eight

The garden was located in a secluded alcove, surrounded on three sides by walls made of bricks chipped and cracked with age. The fourth side consisted of a hedge of shrubbery dense enough to muffle the noise from the street beyond. The sky, momentarily scrubbed clean by last night's rain, formed a brilliant blue canopy over the tiny plot of land. Despite the cool October air, the sun warmed both body and soul. Mary understood why Nathan Garner loved it. His garden was an oasis of serenity.

Except that she didn't feel very serene at the moment. Jake had stripped off his shirt shortly after he'd begun work, and since he'd tersely refused her offer of help, she had little else to do but stare at him—she hoped without his noticing.

He moved with animal-like grace, efficiently lifting and placing each stone. Sweat glistened on skin marred only by a faded scar that started just under his shoulder blade, wrapped around his right side and disappeared beneath his shorts. It lacked the precision of a surgeon's knife, and she shuddered at what that might suggest.

But it was the play of finely honed muscles as he worked that was having the most disturbing effect on her. How could one tank top have hidden so much... masculinity? An insatiable thirst began building inside her, and she didn't know whether to attribute it to the noon heat... or Jake McAlister.

To distract herself, she reached for the thermos of ice water Nathan had left with them. Jake was probably thirsty, too, but she suspected it would be for something a little more practical than what she was envisioning. She poured a cupful and carried it over to him.

"Here," she said, holding out the cup. "Thought you might like a drink."

He finished setting another stone in place, then straightened. "Thanks." Watching her steadily, he took it from her.

His fingers barely brushed hers, but it was enough for her to feel the rough, damp warmth of them. Still watching her, he downed the drink greedily, and liquid heat spiraled through Mary. *Get a grip, girl.*

"Nathan's a delight," she finally said, when she was reasonably sure her voice wouldn't betray her. "I imagine he's used to getting his way a good share of the time."

A half smile came and went. "Yeah, he's a character, all right."

"He must be from around here."

"I don't think so."

"Ah. Then I guess being a minister has its advantages."

Jake raised an eyebrow. "In what way?"

"Apparently you don't include him on your list of outsiders who meddle where they don't belong."

Shrugging, he handed her the empty cup. "Nathan knows what he's doing."

Well, that effectively put an end to the discussion of Nathan Garner. She lifted the thermos. "More?" she asked, searching for another topic.

He nodded, and she took her time refilling the cup.

"Basketball was just what I needed."

He squinted against the bright sun, and she thought she caught a glint of humor. "You looked like you could use a distraction. Shooting hoops is a great way to work off frustration."

She smiled then. "Yes. And I can honestly say I appreciated every minute of it."

He raised an eyebrow. "Considering the score, I guess you did."

"Well, there is that," she said, her smile turning wicked. "But I'm serious. It was very thoughtful of you."

"No problem." He shifted uncomfortably, as if unused to accepting thanks or praise.

"It seems I'm always thanking you for something. I hope at some point I can return the favor."

He saluted her with his cup. "You just did," he said, and again emptied it in one long swallow.

A chuckle escaped her as she took the cup from him and set it and the thermos down. "Somehow I don't think this makes us even."

"No?" He assessed her lazily. "Have you got something better in mind?"

She was close enough to smell the musky scent of him. Close enough to know he wanted to kiss her. She could tell by the way his eyes dilated to black, the way he studied her mouth, the way his body tensed, the way his nostrils flared as if taking in her scent. And she wanted it, too. It seemed the most natural thing in the world, yet at the same time it terrified her.

Jake saw her eyes heat to deep jade. "Look, I'm trying to do the right thing here," he told her gruffly. "You could make it a little easier."

Smiling provocatively she stepped closer. "Why?"

He didn't move to meet her. "Because this isn't a good idea."

It hit her then. Like a splash of ice water, Mary recalled what they'd found last night. "Oh, I see," she said with forced lightness, taking a half step back from him. "You have a problem with me, with who I am." She was unprepared for the amount of pain that voicing the words caused her.

Instantly Jake's right hand shot out, and he hauled her against him. Giving her no chance to object, he brought his mouth down on hers. Hard. At the contact, he groaned deep in his chest. He didn't try to gentle the kiss. He couldn't. The firestorm streaking through his veins wouldn't allow it. It demanded to be fed, and what it craved was this woman.

He tasted of cool water and smelled of sunlight and something erotic, forbidden. Of their own volition, Mary's hands came up to anchor him to her. His heated skin was slippery with perspiration and peppered with grit, and her body arched into his. She couldn't get close enough.

Oh, God, she felt so good. Too good. Jake couldn't remember ever wanting anyone or anything as he wanted this woman at this moment. Not lifting his mouth from hers, he slowly worked his hands down her back to her hips, kneading them, rubbing her against himself. He was ready to explode just holding her, kissing her. The thought of being inside her threatened to push him over the edge.

Some primitive instinct urged him to drag her to the ground, plunge deep inside her and end the sexual torment for both of them. Now. Before he had time to think rationally. Before she could breach any more of his defenses.

That last shred of sanity brought him to his senses. It was almost a replay of the first time he'd kissed her. He forced his mouth from hers. "No," he said on a hoarse laugh, "I don't have a problem with who you are. *That's* my problem."

Still in a sensual daze, Mary had trouble collecting her thoughts. "Then why...?"

He set her away from him, cutting across her words in frustration. "Because I don't have the right. Dammit, *you* don't have the right."

She shook her head, bewildered. "Why wouldn't I have the right to decide who I should kiss?"

"Hasn't it occurred to you that you could be involved with someone back wherever you come from?" Even as he spoke, a hot rage swept through him at the very idea of any other man having a claim on this woman.

Was it possible, Mary wondered, to have experienced these powerful emotions with another man and *not* remember? She couldn't believe it, but apparently Jake did. "If I were seriously involved with someone, wouldn't I feel it? Wouldn't kissing you seem wrong, instead of so damned right?"

Her frankness went straight to Jake's gut, and he groaned. He was treading a narrow edge and he cursed whatever drove him to be so damned honorable. "Careful, sweetheart. My self-control is stretched about as thin as it will go. If you don't leave now, I can't promise I won't end up dragging you to the ground and finishing this right here in the church garden." He laughed sardonically. "Somehow I don't think even you'd thank me for that."

She recognized it as a backhanded compliment, one meant to strike out, to hurt, to drive her away. "Don't I have any say in the matter?"

With nothing coy, nothing devious in mind, she had reached out to him, her emotions open and honest and plain for him to see. It was almost his undoing. Why did he give a damn? he wondered. Why didn't he just take what she was offering, what she wanted, what he sure as hell craved? But for some reason all the rationalization in the world wasn't going to do it. No matter how much he might lust for her, he couldn't take her. Not yet.

"When your memory returns, if you still want this," he promised her, his voice husky, edgy, "we'll make love until neither of us can walk. Now, please, just get the hell out of here."

She looked at him for several seconds longer, not hiding her hurt or confusion. It almost killed him. "All right, Jake. If that's what you want."

Hell, no, it wasn't what he wanted. He watched her turn away, collect her things and go back inside the rectory. He eyed the remaining rocks with new purpose, hoping he could work off his own frustration, knowing he didn't have a prayer in hell of succeeding.

* * *

It didn't take Mary long to locate Nathan Garner. He was in the gym shooting hoops with Will. He played amazingly well, with a style and grace unexpected in such a large man. She inwardly shook her head. He definitely was *not* your average clergyman.

With sandy-colored hair and blue, penetrating eyes, he'd be perfect, she decided, for the romantic lead in some love story. He'd certainly give the current Hollywood heartthrobs a run for their money.

When Nathan spotted her, he hailed her, then sank a one-handed basket. "Come join us."

"Sounds great. Thanks." She was more than ready for another workout, Mary thought wryly as she stripped off her borrowed warm-ups.

Will groaned, retrieving the ball. "You're asking to get beat," he warned Nathan.

"Have a little faith, son."

"Yeah," Will grumbled, grinning, "I have faith she's gonna beat us."

Their laughter was infectious, and the three of them played for fun but not without an undertone of friendly competition. It helped Mary at least get a handle on the jumble of emotions that the past thirty minutes with Jake had stirred in her.

She managed to hold her own against Will and Nathan until the gym door opened and a teenage girl stepped inside. The distraction broke Mary's concentration just enough that her next shot went wide of the basket. Will gleefully capitalized on her lapse, recovering the ball and making the rebound.

"Great timing, Cilla!" Will called to the girl, as the ball swooshed through the frayed net. "Thanks."

"Just remember," Mary pointed out to Will between pants, "you had a little help."

Will sent her a we'll-see-about-that grin and loped over to where the girl called Cilla stood just inside the door, resting her back against the wall. Nathan followed at a slower pace.

Still trying to catch her breath, Mary bent at the waist, braced her hands on her knees and studied the girl. So this was Cilla. She was maybe fourteen or fifteen, and as Will had said, she was beautiful, with large soulful eyes and hair the color of midnight. Her makeup had been applied a bit heavy-handedly, but couldn't mask the air of innocence about her. Or the hint of insecurity.

The three of them started across the room toward the rickety bleachers on the opposite wall. Mary noticed that Cilla seemed to be favoring her right leg. It wasn't much of a limp, and she compensated well. In fact, the length of her flowered slip-dress nearly made it undetectable. But Mary also noticed that Cilla positioned herself beside Will and Nathan so that neither of them were behind her, where they would be able to see her walk.

When they came abreast of Mary, Nathan snagged her elbow. "Come along," he said, drawing her into the little group. "Let's go sit for a few minutes. I, for one, am wiped out." They made their way to the bleachers, Nathan performing the necessary introductions as they went.

"You played real good," Cilla shyly told Mary, a wistful note in her voice. "I was watching through the window for a while before I came in."

It was hard for Mary to tell whether the girl would have any potential as a player. With a limp, it seemed doubtful. "You like basketball?"

Cilla nodded. "I like to watch Will."

"Yeah, for an amateur he's okay." Mary reached around Cilla and gave Will a friendly poke. But instead of countering the playful gesture, Will put a protective arm around the girl, as if wanting to keep her from being jostled.

Seating herself on a bench, Cilla turned adoring eyes on Will. "He's better than okay," she defended firmly. "He's number one on the school team."

"Is that right?" Mary tried to look properly chastised, while fighting to keep from laughing at Will's chagrined expression. "He failed to mention that earlier."

Nathan pulled Mary's arm through the crook of his own. "How about a cup of freshly brewed tea, Mary?"

"I'd love one." Mary was surprised at just how good that sounded. She quickly slipped into her sweats, and Nathan sent her an unspoken signal to follow him. She complied, but Will and Cilla, already tuned in to each other, remained seated.

Once out of earshot, Nathan explained. "I wanted to give them a little time to themselves. This is the only place they can meet without causing her family too much grief."

She glanced back over her shoulder at the two teenagers, sitting side by side on the bench, deep in conversation. "You mean this meeting was prearranged?"

"Not exactly. There's a pretty good grapevine in the community. If you want to get a message out, it's not too difficult."

Her mouth twitched. "You sure it's wise leaving them alone?"

"Ah, Mary," Nathan said, the corners of his eyes crinkling. "Haven't you figured it out? Will's appointed himself Cilla's champion. She'll be safe with him."

She looked back at Will, saw the longing in his face as he listened intently to something Cilla was saying. "I'll take your word for it." Nathan ushered Mary through the gym door and into the hall. "What's wrong with her leg?"

"She was born with a club foot."

"Can't it be corrected?"

Nathan shook his head. "Her family can't afford the surgery."

She sent him a puzzled look. "Aren't there agencies to take care of that?"

"Yes. But you have to understand, Cilla's family is very proud."

"That's a shame. She's very self-conscious about it."

"You noticed," he said, and seemed impressed that she had. "I worry about her. Cilla tries hard to hide it, but a girl her age yearns for the acceptance and approval of her peers."

What was it Will had said about gangs and his concern for Cilla? Something about their being like family? Cilla's limp would make her susceptible to attention from other guys and even more so to the influence of a gang, Mary realized with a frown, particularly if its members used acceptance as the lure.

They reached the church kitchen, and Nathan gestured for Mary to take one of the stools in front of the waist-high counter. The Formica on the countertop was so stained and chipped that it was difficult to tell what color it had originally been. All the same, it was scrupulously clean.

"Have a seat. It won't take me a minute to get the tea started." He collected cups, loose tea, sugar and lemon, then sat on the stool next to Mary while they waited for the water to boil.

Nathan propped his elbows on the counter and pinned her with an assessing look, almost as penetrating as Jake's. "Did Jake run into a problem in the garden?" he asked casually. "I didn't expect this little project would take quite so long."

Remembering the cause of the delay, she felt her cheeks warm. "Well . . . not exactly."

A twinkle appeared in Nathan's eyes. "Does that mean you were a distraction?"

The unexpected statement coming from a man of the cloth startled her. "Was that your plan?"

He shrugged, his expression becoming a model of innocence. "Jake could use some distraction in his life." Just then the kettle announced its readiness, and he went to retrieve it.

"Have you known him long, Nathan?"

"Going on three years." He poured water over the waiting tea leaves. "Long enough that he's learned to tolerate me. Early on he wouldn't have any part of us."

"That's the Jake I've come to know and—" she broke off, mentally shying away from what usually followed "—care for," she finished.

"He has good reason," he said. "From the little I've learned about him, I imagine he feels everyone, including God, deserted him and his sister when they needed them most. People have to prove themselves to Jake first. And that isn't an easy task."

Mary's heart ached. It was much too easy to imagine how what had happened to Debbie could teach a younger Jake to turn away from everyone, trust no one. "Not to mention that he considers anyone not born and raised here an outsider and by that fact suspect," she said, half to herself. She reached for her tea, surprised how soothing the aroma seemed, and automatically added sugar.

Nathan regarded her speculatively for several seconds. "That's very perceptive of you. Not too many people understand that."

"Yes, well," she said in self-mockery, "I seem to understand all kinds of things lately."

Sympathy softened Nathan's features. "I'm here, Mary, if you'd like to talk."

Mary swallowed to get past the fresh wave of frustration clogging her throat. "Thanks. I may take you up on that—as soon as I have something to talk about."

"Drink your tea," he instructed, his voice containing empathy and something else she couldn't name. "Someone once told me that a strong cup of tea could solve a good share of our troubles if we'd only let it."

Doubtful, she took a sip. The liquid was hot enough to scald her tongue, but it was the first tang of unique spices that sparked an immediate and vivid image in her mind's eye.

She was sitting on another stool in another kitchen, sipping tea. But that room was ultramodern and equipped with the latest in expensive culinary gadgets. Across the counter from her sat a woman, a few years older. She had beautiful expressive eyes, eyes filled with caring and warmth and concern.

The breath froze in Mary's chest. She knew the woman's name. It was familiar and dear to her. Her brain seemed to burn as it struggled to sort through and identify the swift flow of memory fragments.

Her sister! Stephanie Victoria Harcourt—except Stephie was married now and her last name was...Saxon. The revelation hit her like an electrical current touched to a wet surface. How many times had her sister and she sat drinking this exact brand of tea and talking over whatever was troubling them?

She was vaguely conscious of someone urgently speaking her name. No, not Mary, she recalled, but she remained silent. *Alex* . . . her name was Alex. Her head throbbed with the effort to remember all of it. *Ashley Alexandra Harcourt.*

The touch of a gentle hand on her arm jolted Alex back to the present. Nathan was regarding her with concern.

"Sorry. What did you say?" she asked, trying to keep a bubble of hysterical laughter from escaping. Tea! A simple cup of tea was responsible for returning her memory. Apparently at some point she'd set her cup down. Now she wrapped her hands around it to keep them from shaking.

"I asked if you're all right. You've gone pale."

She lifted a hand to rub her forehead, searching for a believable excuse. "Maybe I overdid today. I feel...a bit strange." She stood. "If you'll excuse me, I think I'll go to the ladies' room."

"Are you certain you can make it by yourself?" Nathan asked, still watching her closely, a frown shadowing his strong features.

Assuring him she'd be fine, she hurried from the kitchen. She needed a few minutes alone, time to absorb the overwhelming reality of what was happening to her. Time to sort through the multitude of emotions assaulting her.

In the bathroom she went straight to the sink. She splashed water on her face before examining it in the cracked mirror. The memories were coming faster now. Some were still hazy, but others emerged complete, in minute detail. Whole chunks of her past, filled the blank spaces that had haunted her for days. Scenes from her childhood. Reading stories to her nephew...Jason. But as yet, only vague recollections about more recent events.

She forced herself to take a deep steadying breath. She wasn't ready to share this with anyone. But she needed to get back. If she didn't soon, Nathan was sure to come looking for her. She sensed that he was nearly as protective as Jake.

Besides, she wanted to find out what she could about Jake from Nathan. Squaring her shoulders, she retraced her steps to the kitchen.

The first person Alex encountered when she reentered the kitchen was Jake. He was sitting on the stool she'd vacated a short while ago—no, make that a lifetime ago—cradling a mug of tea between his palms.

He looked up as she walked in, his expression wary but intent. "You okay?"

She experienced a moment of confusion, followed by a blur of fresh images. She'd seen that same uncompromising look on Jake's face that night. In the alley. Bits and pieces of memory rushed in on her. Danger... men talking... a familiar voice... a drug deal... Drug deal? The rational part of her mind froze.

Say something, Alex ordered herself, *he's expecting a response.* The last thing she needed was to give herself away, at least not until she'd had a chance to come to terms with all that was happening to her. "I'm fine," she said, schooling her features into neutrality. "Nothing major. Even with Will's help, beating you this morning must have taken more out of me than I realized." She recognized it was a weak attempt at humor.

He continued to assess her, much as an astronomer might assess some dark secret in the far reaches of the universe through a telescope. He was searching, Alex was convinced, for some indication that she was lying.

The hint of a smile pulled at his mouth. "Wouldn't hurt for you to remember that the next time you challenge me."

She returned his smile, hoping it looked natural. "Believe me, I will."

"Take her home, Jake," Nathan advised. "She should rest."

Jake stood, still studying her. "You're right. Let's round up Will and get out of here."

Except Alex now realized that Jake couldn't take her home. He didn't know where she lived. Her home was... She struggled to connect the fragments of information floating through her consciousness. Her home was...miles from here. In a very safe neighborhood, a very *rich* neighborhood. The kind Jake had no use for, filled with people Jake wanted no part of. A void yawned inside her, a new one she feared would be with her for a very long time.

She couldn't dwell on that now. *Finish it,* she silently instructed, *remember it all.* Then she could decide what to do about it, how to handle it. What— and what not—to tell Jake.

Why was she here in his territory dressed as a hooker? Why had she been in the alley that night? But that information stubbornly refused to emerge. Frustration and a sense of dread threatened to overwhelm her. It was almost as if she didn't want to remember.

Thankfully, neither Jake nor Will seemed interested in conversation on the ride back to Sondra's. It gave Alex precious minutes to get herself under firm control before they reached the small house.

As they waited for a green light, her attention was drawn to a woman and man lingering in a doorway out of the flow of other pedestrians. Alex found herself absently studying the couple.

Judging by her bizarre get-up, the woman had to be a working girl. Was the man a potential customer? No, Alex decided, the woman didn't look as if she was soliciting. She looked...frightened, yet a bit defiant. The man was a sharp dresser in a sleazy sort of way—as if he had more money than taste. More likely he was her pimp. Why had she even noticed the couple, Alex wondered, much less formed an opinion about their identities?

Comprehension came like a crack of thunder. She wasn't analyzing the situation from personal experience but from professional training. Police training. She wasn't a hooker... She was a cop, a cop who was working undercover as a prostitute. The relief washing over Alex was so great that it almost took her breath away. But close on its heels came a new concern.

Her assignment had been to locate and identify the source of drugs being funneled into the suburban area north of D.C. The reason she'd gone to the alley was to follow up on a tip, a tip regarding a possible drug deal going down that night.

So what had Jake been doing there?

Something niggled at the fringes of her memory. She'd shied away from it earlier; now she forced herself to concentrate, to bring it into focus.

The alley was dark, only a dim light burning at the opposite end. It made seeing difficult, doubly so considering three of the four men present were out of her line of vision. Only two of them were actually engaged in conversation, and from her position behind the wooden crates Alex was having equal difficulty hearing. She strained to pick up their words.

"I understand you're the best in the business, McAlister," said the man whose voice had the ring of education and privilege. *"I'm willing to offer you exclusive rights to the northwestern territory."*

Something about this guy disturbed Alex. His voice sounded... familiar.

"And what's my end of this deal?" the man called McAlister asked.

He was the only one of the four Alex had a clear view of. In the dim light he appeared commanding, dangerous. And she sensed, without understanding why, that he'd be relentless in getting a job done. She shivered and carefully inched closer. The unsteady crate protecting her moved precariously. Holding her breath, she prayed she hadn't given herself away. She glanced at McAlister. He seemed to be staring straight at her. Her heart kicked into overdrive.

"Am I boring you, Mr. McAlister?"

McAlister's attention shifted back to the man. "Just thinking over your offer, Brady."

Brady? In that instant Alex put it together. She should have caught on the first time she heard him speak with just that touch of snobbish condescension. My God, she thought frantically, this was George Brady. An old family acquaintance. A man she'd known most of her life. And he'd just offered the man called McAlister exclusive rights to deal drugs in one of the most prestigious suburban territories outside D.C.

Then all hell broke loose and everything went black.

Chapter Nine

Was Jake McAlister a drug dealer?

Though there was a part of her that couldn't believe it, Alex's immediate instinct was to flee. At the next stoplight, all she had to do was open the car door and run like hell. But her professional training precluded that option. Jake was already watching her questioningly, his sharp senses obviously picking up on her agitation.

She had to get away from him. Away from the tangible threat he posed to her cover. Away from the emotional threat he posed to her heart. Back to safety, back to the welcoming arms of her family. But she had to do it without raising suspicion. Alex concentrated on bringing her breathing into normal range.

Stephie had to be frantic by now. Not to mention Alex's superior at the department. Bob Griffin would be damning her and calling himself every kind of fool for letting her talk him into working this case without a partner.

By the time Jake stopped the car in front of Sondra's, a professional calm had settled over Alex. She knew what had to be done, and by wrapping all her training and experience around her like a shield, she'd do it. Until then she'd play her expected role. Concentrating on that went a long way toward steadying her shaky nerves.

Jake dropped Will and Alex off at the crumbling cement curb in front of the row house and went to stash the car wherever it was he kept it.

As they climbed the old marble steps to the front door, Alex studied Will to keep her mind off her own dilemma. Even for Will, he was unusually silent. He seemed preoccupied. No, more than preoccupied— something was troubling him. She sighed inwardly. Like it or not, she'd come to care for the kid. And no matter how unwise it was, she wanted to help him. She wondered, once all this was over, if she'd have the chance.

"I'm glad to have met Cilla," she said to break the silence.

Will half smiled for the first time since they'd left the church. "She likes you."

"I like her, too," Alex said, unlocking the door with the key Jake had handed her as she'd climbed out of the car. She opened it, stepped back so Will could enter, then followed him inside. "Did you two have a nice visit?"

"It was okay." Shoulders stiff, he shoved his hands into his pockets. "Except she told me she's really serious about hooking up with this gang."

By unspoken decision, they headed for the kitchen, Alex searching for something that might ease Will's distress. Not to mention her own. "Sometimes," Alex said carefully, "the only thing we can do for the people we care about is let them make their own decisions. Even when we know it's bad for them. Even when it hurts."

He shook his head. "But she doesn't know what she's getting into," he said, desperation edging his words.

But Will obviously knew, and he was frightened for Cilla. He'd hinted at some of it when he and Alex had talked before. There was nothing she could say to lessen his concern; her only other option was to encourage him to talk. Though far from hungry, she went to the refrigerator and began gathering the makings for sandwiches. At least it gave her something to do.

"She's going to get in a crap-load of trouble and nobody's gonna be there to help her." Will slammed his fist against the counter, causing Alex to flinch. "If Jake didn't have such an attitude about the gang," he added in frustration, "I'd go with her. Then I could look out for her."

"You think that'd be a smart move?" she asked. "Wouldn't that put you in as much danger as she's in?"

"I can take care of myself," he assured her flatly, then began to prowl the small room. The leashed energy emanating from him reminded Alex of Jake. "But I guess you're right. It probably wouldn't be so smart."

Alex nodded her approval. On one hand, learning that Will apparently had listened to at least part of what Jake had tried to get across to him alleviated some of Alex's concern. On the other, realizing that Will felt he was being backed into a corner alarmed her. She searched for another solution, one that wouldn't put both these young people at risk. "Has Cilla made the decision yet, or is she just thinking about it?"

One shoulder lifted. "She says she's still thinking. But I know it's just a matter of time."

"Can you keep her thinking awhile longer?"

"Thinking about what?" Jake asked from the kitchen doorway.

Alex jumped, and Will jerked around to stare uncomfortably at the man entering the room. "Uh, nothing important." Will began inching toward the door Jake had just entered. "I gotta go," he said and was down the hall in two blinks.

"Will, wait a minute," Alex called after him.

Hands on his hips, Jake sighed. "Let him go," he said. He rubbed the back of his neck, demonstrating his own frustration. "He's not going to talk about whatever's bothering him until he's ready."

She should've guessed that Jake would notice something was troubling Will. And that it would worry him. Frowning, Alex walked down the hall to peer out the front window, acutely conscious that Jake had followed her.

"Where will he go?" she asked, watching the tall teenager jog down the street until he was out of sight. Sensing Jake's presence close enough that she could feel his body heat, she turned to face him. "Does he have someone at home he can talk to?"

Jake snorted scornfully. "A mother, if you can call her that. Most of the time she's drunk. Or worse. If she talks at all, it's to remind Will what a damned burden he is.''

Her heart went out to this teenager, left alone to handle problems that would seem daunting even to an adult. ''Doesn't he have other relatives?''

Jake shook his head.

''Then who looks out for Will?''

For a brief moment worry flickered in Jake's eyes. ''Pretty much he's on his own.''

The similarity between Will's childhood and Jake's squeezed at Alex's chest. ''When you have troubles the size of his, I imagine friends are important.''

''Friends can cause a helluva lot more problems than they solve.'' Jake's implacable words stated clearly his belief that there was no other side to the discussion.

''But a good friend could be his salvation,'' she countered quietly.

Jake sent her a challenging look.

''You, for instance.''

He shrugged away her observation. ''He'd be better off if he learned to take care of himself, be a survivor. Then he won't need anyone else.''

That comment, as none other could, convinced Alex that Jake saw himself in Will. That, whether he admitted it or not, he wanted to spare Will the pain he'd endured. And her heart ached for Jake, for both of them, because she knew it was history repeating itself. If no one intervened, he'd teach Will to distance himself from everyone, to train himself to allow no one close enough to hurt him.

''Does that include girlfriends?'' she asked, wondering if she were stepping into quicksand. She took a deep breath and plunged ahead anyway. "I met Cilla today."

That obviously surprised Jake. The muscle in his jaw bunched in displeasure. "Will introduced you?"

Loath to get Will into hot water, she hedged. "Actually, Nathan introduced us." That much was true. There was no law that said she had to tell Jake everything, was there? "She's a beautiful girl. And sweet."

"Yeah. Just the kind a kid like Will doesn't need."

Alex pursed her lips and looked at him consideringly. "Because she's beautiful or because she's sweet?"

Jake chuckled, but the sound held an underlying note she couldn't identify. "Both. Sweet or beautiful, women have been tempting men since the Garden of Eden."

She raised an eyebrow. "Jake McAlister, that's blatantly sexist." His grin broadened. "What about a man tempting a woman?" she challenged indignantly.

His smile grew lazy. "Want to give me an example?" he said, his voice dropping an octave.

A ripple of excitement curled through Alex and settled in a warm ache low in her body. Something told her that flirting with Jake McAlister was about as smart as teasing a predatory animal. It might be exciting but it left her vulnerable to losing some vital part of herself. She decided sticking to the original subject was definitely safer. "It's a shame about Cilla's foot."

Alex glimpsed a touch of sympathy in Jake's eyes, but a heartbeat later he neutralized it. "Yeah. Life hands out tough breaks."

She bit her lip. How far could she push this before Jake told her in no uncertain terms to mind her own business? "I think Will wants to help her."

Without changing his stance, the relaxed Jake was gone and in his place was the unyielding loner. "I don't need you to tell me what Will wants. Or needs."

"She should have surgery," Alex persisted, refusing to be intimidated or to let his words hurt. "Nathan told me her family couldn't afford it. Maybe we could find a way to raise the money."

If she hadn't come to know him during the past several days, the transformation in Jake might have been terrifying. He rounded on her, his eyes cold, hard, furious. "Don't put ideas in Will's head," he said, his voice low. "Don't make him hope for things he can't have. As soon as your memory returns, you'll be gone and he'll be left with nothing but good intentions. I can tell you from bitter experience, they give cold comfort in the dead of night."

Even though she understood what prompted them, this time Jake's words found their mark, sliced deep. "You'll find that I have a tendency to speak my mind. That when I see something that needs doing, I don't run from it." She gave him a level look. "And that I never make promises lightly."

He stared at her for a good ten seconds. "How the hell would you know?"

Holding her breath, Alex steadily returned his stare. A frown drew his dark brows together, and she could almost see his brain analyzing what she'd said.

"You remember." It wasn't a question.

She nodded, wondering if she'd made a huge mistake confirming that her memory had returned.

Looking as if he'd had the wind knocked out of him, he ran a hand through his hair. "All of it?"

Again she nodded. This was the first time she'd seen him flustered, and, oddly, it made her simultaneously want to laugh and cry.

He crossed the room and stopped beside her. Placing a hand on her shoulders, he turned her to face him. She was acutely conscious of his controlled strength. "Are you okay?" he asked, studying her carefully.

She smiled uncertainly. "As okay as I can be for someone who's had her entire life history dumped into her head in one overwhelming chunk."

Jake's eyes warmed again, but the frown still shadowed his forehead. He continued to study her for several heartbeats, his eyes searching. But his expression made her believe that he was as relieved as she that her ordeal was over. "Even so, you gotta feel like you've been let out of a dark cellar."

"Good comparison." Speaking around the lump in her throat wasn't easy. "But it wouldn't have happened without help," she told him softly. "Will's, Nathan's. Yours. We all need a helping hand sometime. It's terrifyingly lonely to have no one but yourself."

His hands dropped away from her shoulders, and the warmth faded from his eyes. The sudden loss left her feeling bereft.

"But a damned sight safer," he told her. "Don't interfere where you don't belong."

"How do you know I don't belong here?"

"Do you?"

Alex returned his stare, feeling as if she were drowning and he possessed the only life raft. "Do you really want to know?" she challenged softly.

Jake didn't like the mix of emotions poking holes in his gut. He wasn't ready for this. Did he want to know who she was, where she came from? If there was a lover waiting for her? If he could handle her leaving without a backward glance? The fact that he cared at all left him feeling exposed. "All I want you to tell me," he said succinctly, "is what the hell you were doing in the alley."

Suddenly, Alex had the illogical urge to give Jake what he wanted, to tell him everything. She might have witnessed Jake McAlister talking a drug deal, but she'd never heard him accept. All she'd seen or heard was his asking George Brady for more details. She'd used the same stalling tactics herself more than once.

Of course, her shrewd mind argued, Jake could have accepted Brady's offer while she was out cold on the cement. True, she countered, but if he were a drug dealer, how did she explain all the good she'd witnessed in this man during the short time she'd known him?

How did she reconcile the dangerous, uncompromising man she remembered from that night in the alley with the Jake McAlister she'd gotten to know over the past several days? The one who'd tended her wounds, showed gruff-gentle consideration for her terror caused by the amnesia, treated her with respect and as an equal, even though he had reason to believe her a common hooker.

And how did she explain his affection for a street kid? His willingness to help out a minister. His anguish over the fate of a long-dead sister, snatched from him when he was much too young. In fact, Alex hadn't witnessed Jake do a single thing that could be considered threatening or harmful to anyone. Except maybe himself. Not usual traits found in a criminal.

Something else was going on here. Jake McAlister simply could not be what he apparently wanted people to believe. No matter what her eyes and ears might have witnessed that night, there had to be some other explanation. She knew deep down that any secret she shared with this man would be safe.

But her rigid training won out. There were other people involved, and no matter how certain she might be, she hadn't the right to make that decision for them. Sooner or later she'd get to the bottom of it. But now was not the right time. Telling Jake the whole truth about herself was out. Bottom line, she had to protect her cover.

Her best option, she decided, was to stick as close to the truth as possible without divulging sensitive information. She'd never learned to lie comfortably, even when playing a role. Now, lying about herself she found doubly hard.

She became aware that her hands were clammy cold. In a rush it came to her that this was the one physical manifestation of fear she'd never conquered. Wrapping her arms around herself, she tucked her hands against her sides and moved to the other side of the room, away from Jake. That way she didn't have to look him in the eye.

"I was on my way to...work," she began, "when I noticed a stray cat run into the alley. It was such a pathetic little thing that I couldn't bear to walk away from it. So I followed, hoping to find it. Next thing I know, four men are using the area for a chat session." She felt Jake's sharp gaze boring into her, weighing her words, judging her veracity.

"And how much did you hear?"

"For Pete's sake!" Alex exclaimed, throwing her hands up. "I was crouched behind a bunch of boxes." Hating the fabrication, she turned his question back on him. "What the hell do you think I heard?"

He continued assessing her, searching for holes in her story. Or a chink in her armor? "All right," he said after what seemed an interminable length of time. "Tell me who you are."

Don't ask, she silently begged. *You won't like the answer.* Something told her he'd probably prefer her to be the hooker they'd thought rather than learn who she really was—a member of the elite social set of Washington, D.C. It would be funny if it didn't hurt so much.

"I thought we'd established that the other night. What you see is what you get," she said, hoping as she uttered it that he'd see beneath the lie to the real Alexandra Harcourt. Suddenly feeling exposed, she hugged herself tighter and turned away.

So it was true. The disappointment that sliced into Jake cut deep, much deeper than he cared to admit. The fact that she was a hooker shouldn't matter, but it did. And he hated it. "And I'll bet Mary isn't your real name."

She shook her head. "Alex," she said, deliberately holding back her last name.

He walked over to her, stopping within touching distance. "Short for Alexandra, right?"

Alex nodded, her heart beginning to pound inside her chest.

A corner of his mouth curved, and he ran a finger down her cheek. "I knew you had royalty in you."

Sexual awareness, sharp and sweet, crackled between them, increasing the ache deep inside Alex. She'd come to care for this man far more than was good for her heart. She was in big trouble. Could she marshal the strength needed to walk away from him?

"Is that all you're going to tell me?"

"I guarantee you know everything about me that's important."

Something like sadness tore at Jake. He let his gaze wander over her face. "You don't have to live this way."

Alex didn't pretend to misunderstand. The emotional part of her wanted to rail at him for even entertaining the thought that she could be a prostitute, while the rational part reminded her that was exactly what he was supposed to think. Though tears stung her eyes, she smiled provocatively. "Ah, I see. You doubt I'm good at what I do?"

"Oh, honey," he said, his voice growing husky, "I'm certain you're better than good. But that's not what I'm talking about here. You're a beautiful woman. And smart. There are other ways to make a living."

"Hmm. Beautiful and smart. Nice." But the compliment tasted bittersweet. Oh yes, she knew she was beautiful. Hadn't countless people told her so over her lifetime? Why had she allowed herself to hope Jake would see something besides surface beauty in her? "In other words, get an honest job?"

He frowned, momentarily disconcerted. "What I'm saying is that you have a lot going for you. You're good with people, a great listener." The amount of personal information she'd been able to get out of him still amazed Jake. "Getting Will to say more than four words at one time was no small feat."

She felt shackled by her lies. A part of her conceded that she could tell him she wasn't a hooker and still protect her cover. She could tell him she was a waitress in some dive or just a woman who liked provocative clothes. But then she'd risk opening up the discussion to more questions. More lies. There was no way she could safely dispel his misconception. It was better to continue to play her role.

Finding it increasingly difficult to soothe the ache inside her, she smiled brightly. "Ah. With those stellar traits, I could always become a social worker."

Suddenly she seemed too smooth, Jake noticed. He couldn't seem to catch her off guard and he was an expert at that. Something savage knifed through Jake. Hearing her make light of her circumstances did odd things to him. Things he didn't want to examine too closely. "Don't," he said roughly. "Don't joke about this. About yourself." He moved closer to her and framed her face with his hands.

Jake's fierce tenderness coupled with the anger Alex sensed just beneath the surface fired her blood and sent her pulse racing. She was a professional, she reminded herself. She was supposed to remain objective, to control the situation. Not let the situation control her.

But she couldn't ignore Jake's nearness, his heat, the musky scent of him. She'd learned, from unhappy experiences with the few men she'd felt any attraction toward, to control the urge, to keep her relationships on a superficial footing. That fact alone made the man gently cradling her face unique. When he was around, she couldn't seem to keep her mind from wandering into areas best left unexplored.

She'd mastered the art of acting flamboyant and self-assured around others, but she'd always protected her emotions, made certain she did nothing that might leave her vulnerable. Some feminine instinct told her that this man was different. That if she backed away from this, she'd regret it for the rest of her life.

From the beginning, she'd responded differently to Jake McAlister than to any man before him. It frightened her while making her want to explore the reasons why. Against her better judgment, she'd wanted him when she'd had no memory of who she was. Regaining her memory hadn't diminished that. If anything, the longing had increased.

No matter what her role, no matter who this man was, she wanted to experience all she could with him. In a few short hours, she'd be gone. And she intended to take all the memories possible with her.

Her smile faded, and she leaned into Jake. "I believe," she said, surprised at how unsteady her voice sounded, "you promised me that when my memory returned, you'd finish what we started in the garden."

Chapter Ten

Desire, swift and hot, surged through Jake, and coherent thought fled in the face of Alex's sweetly provocative challenge. He'd never confronted anyone quite like her. Tomorrow they would talk. Tomorrow he'd figure out how to deal with the damage this woman had done to his defenses.

Keeping his raging hormones under tight rein the past several days had put one hell of a strain on his self-control. But he'd had a hunch—or had he simply hoped?—that it wouldn't be wise to act on circumstantial evidence alone. That there was still the possibility she might not be what she appeared.

He wondered what kind of fool that made him. He pushed the troubling thought to a distant corner of his mind. Now he only wanted to concentrate on Alex. There was no reason not to take what she was offering, what he so desperately hungered for. But he wanted it his way.

It took a minute for his pounding heartbeat to settle enough for him to keep his voice steady. "Do you remember the other condition?"

"I assure you," Alex told him, her voice quiet, her smoky gaze steady, "I've forgotten nothing about this afternoon."

Jake slid both hands into her hair, flexing them, holding her prisoner. "Then say it," he demanded, aware there was a raw edge to his words. "Tell me you want me."

He watched confusion enter her eyes. They were such a clear fathomless green that a man could almost be duped into believing she'd never experienced the seamier side of life, that she hid no dark secrets.

"Can you doubt it?" she asked huskily.

"Then give me the words."

"I want you, Jake McAlister." Her arms encircled his waist and she pressed her breasts against his chest. Even through her sweatshirt and his thinner shirt, Jake felt her aroused nipples. She ran her tongue over her lips before she spoke, as if she was having as much difficulty as he. That gave him a great deal of satisfaction.

He lowered his mouth until it was a scant inch from hers. "Good, because I want the real thing—the real woman, the real Alex." Jake recalled that she hadn't offered her last name and it made him edgy. The suspicious part of him urged him to demand that she tell him everything, leave out nothing. But desire was clouding his senses. Later, he silently pledged. He'd find out what he needed to know later.

The feel of Jake's strong hands bracketing her face and his intense gaze shook Alex to the core. She sensed a potential for caring in Jake as broad and as deep as the loneliness he so closely guarded. She'd grown to understand him so well... too well. If she wasn't careful, she was going to reveal more to this man than was wise.

Was she making the mistake of a lifetime? Could she make love with Jake and still protect the most vulnerable part of herself? She bolstered her defenses and prayed it wouldn't include her heart.

"I'll give you everything I can," she promised. Unwise though it might be, she intended to commit to memory every vivid detail of her time with Jake McAlister.

Calling on his last ounce of restraint, he slowly lowered his head to hers, giving her one last chance to pull away, pleading with the fates that she wouldn't. She didn't disappoint him. She lifted her mouth the last few millimeters to eagerly accept his.

She'd said she was experienced. And her first kiss was. It was hot and wet and utterly uninhibited, and Jake tried to tell himself that was all he needed tonight.

When he raised his head to look down at her, he ran his hand slowly up her throat until he reached her soft lower lip and gently rubbed its moist fullness. "I want to take this slow," he told her unevenly, his breath rasping in his throat. "Otherwise it will be over before I have a chance to get to know you... and your body. And I intend to do both."

Oh, God, Alex wondered frantically, *how am I going to handle this?* She'd prayed he'd be quick, quick enough that he wouldn't notice she was anything but an expert in lovemaking. Quick enough that she could hide just how much her emotions were involved.

In the past she'd relied on flip remarks as an effective way to keep men at bay. It had always worked well in professional or social settings. She'd never allowed herself to get trapped in an intimate situation she didn't feel capable of controlling. Until now.

"Nothing else matters now. This is just about you—" he drew his hand away from her face, slid it slowly to the sensitive area between her breasts and lightly massaged "—and me—" he took her hand, placed it on his chest and held it there "—making love."

The heavy beat of his heart against her palm sent a streak of heat curling through Alex. Jake was tearing down her defense, touch by seductive touch. He was stripping her bare, and all she could do was hang on to him and hope she didn't drown in the eroticism.

He settled his mouth over hers again, this time with soft, slow sensuality, this time tenderly—making the effect all the more devastating for it.

Jake sensed her panic but refused to let it sway him. It required all his willpower, but he took his time, deepening the kiss, thoroughly exploring her mouth, testing its textures, savoring her taste. His hand came up to cup one exquisite breast, gently teasing the nipple through the heavy fabric of her sweatshirt, and she made a small pleading sound deep in her throat.

She no longer seemed sure of herself. Instead, she seemed almost...chaste. And it turned Jake on as no aphrodisiac possibly could. A power, primitive and possessive, unlike any he'd ever experienced before, fired his blood.

There was something tentative about her now, about the way she approached the kiss, as if she wasn't certain she knew how to please him.

He lifted his mouth from hers just enough to speak. "I want it all, Alex. Just you and me. No barriers. No pretenses."

Alex felt the last of her reserves crumble, and she gave herself over to him. This was what she wanted, she reminded herself. Memories. As many as she could make. Later she'd worry about the consequences.

Instantly aware of her capitulation, Jake refused to acknowledge the twinge of conscience that questioned what gave him the right to push Alex. Driven by a basic impulse so strong that it couldn't be denied, he lifted her and carried her up the stairs to the small bedroom. He kicked the door closed behind him, walked to the bed, then set her on her feet beside it. She swayed slightly and grabbed for his shoulders.

"Easy, honey." He framed her face with his hands. She looked dazed—and so damned vulnerable. He'd show her another side of lovemaking, he vowed. Impulsive and absorbed and ... caring.

He didn't want to analyze why it had become so critical that he make this experience with Alex more than just sex. He'd never given it much thought with any other woman. Sex had always been the mutual satisfaction of a carnal urge, and only between two consenting adults who understood the rules up-front. He'd always made certain it was nothing more. But he desperately wanted to make this time special for this woman.

"Let's take it slow, sweetheart." He lowered his head to hers and her mouth opened eagerly to receive his. She moaned as the kiss grew hotter, more demanding. Freeing her mouth, he stepped back far enough to remove her sweatshirt and discard it.

She wasn't wearing a bra. Seeing her exquisite breasts bare for the first time almost took his breath away. "I've never seen anyone as beautiful as you."

"No," she said, placing her fingers over his lips. "No compliments."

Surprised, Jake searched her face. He tugged her hand away. "Why not? You must know you're one of the most beautiful women in the world."

"But I had nothing to do with it. It's simply the right combination of genes." She shrugged. "It has nothing to do with who I am, what I am inside."

He searched her face. "No. But your beauty is part of you," he said softly. "It's one of the things that makes you Alex." He lightly stroked one nipple, then the other. They instantly puckered in response, and he felt a primal pleasure spread through him. Lowering his head, he followed his fingers with his tongue.

Alex made a small sound in the back of her throat that could have been either denial or encouragement. But her head fell back, as if she relished the feel of his tongue on her delicate flesh.

Her smell wrapped around him, drawing him in, calling to some elemental part of him. He lifted his head to study her expression. It was drowsy with arousal.

"I love your smell." Burying his face between her breasts, he inhaled deeply. "It was one of the first things I noticed about you," he breathed against her heated skin. Her perfume, the distinct scent of her, had teased him ever since he'd become conscious of it after tackling her in the alley. It aroused him, but more, it played havoc with his rational thinking. And he knew, deep inside, that it was permanently imprinted on his senses, that he'd never be able to erase it from his memory.

She opened her eyes and slowly focused on his face. "The first thing I remember about you," she said with difficulty, "was wondering whether you represented danger or safety."

His eyes glittered. "And have you decided?"

"No," she told him truthfully.

He muttered something she couldn't decipher just before he took her other nipple into his mouth and suckled deeply. Coherent thought fled, and she slid her hands into his hair to hold him to her.

Jake couldn't seem to get close enough to her. He wanted her out of her clothes, wanted nothing between them. He lifted his head and tried to get her sweatpants off. But he found himself fumbling. Funny, he didn't recall being nervous with women before.

When she stood naked before him, his breath lodged in his lungs. But it wasn't the sight of her body that overwhelmed him. It was the open, honest desire on her face that she made no attempt to hide.

"You're so... incredibly beautiful," he said roughly, trying to control the violent need shaking him.

Alex placed her fingers over his mouth, stopping the words she didn't want to hear. She sensed Jake's struggle for control. And she resented it. Why should he be exempt from the chaotic emotions that were buffeting her?

She ran her hands up under his shirt, caressing his skin. "I want to see you," she said, pulling the shirt over his head. Her hands went to the button on his waistband. It took a couple of tries, but she finally got it undone and slowly lowered the zipper.

When she took him into her hand, Jake's breath came out in a harsh groan. "God...honey..." He stilled her hand, knowing he was at his limit. He felt raw, exposed.

Pulling her to the bed with him, he rolled over her, fusing his mouth to hers. Concerned he might be hurting her, he tried to gentle the kiss, but she protested, answering his passion with equal intensity.

It was the final challenge to his control. Nothing mattered now but being inside Alex. Some still-sane corner of his mind told him he had to protect her. Reaching across her, he opened the drawer and groped for a condom.

The need driving him shook him to his soul. But he'd worry about that later. Now...now he wanted to feast on her, try to satisfy his craving for this woman. Maybe it would be enough.

Jake settled Alex possessively against his left side, and she waited for her breathing to return to normal. But Alex seriously doubted anything would ever again be normal for her.

He absently stroked her rib cage, and she shivered in delayed reaction. "Will you let me help you?" His words fell into the silence of the twilight-lit bedroom.

Still dazed by their lovemaking, Alex found herself listening more to the deep timbre of Jake's voice than to the actual words. It sounded mesmerizing, comforting and most of all, caring. "Umm," she said, listening to the heavy beat of his heart. "Help me how?"

"I have a few connections. Let me help you get a respec—" Jake broke off when he realized he was about to say respectable. "Job?"

He knew he shouldn't pursue this now, should simply revel in Alex's exquisite body and forget everything else. But he couldn't silence the part of him that admired the fierce independence he'd noticed in her from their first meeting. The vulnerability she so carefully tried to conceal with her spunk and courage aroused his protective instincts and made him want to take care of her.

Jake's meaning finally penetrated Alex's sensual haze. While one part of her found his concern for her immeasurably touching, another part couldn't help taking offense. After what they'd just shared, couldn't he see the person she really was? Was he, like so many others, to judge her by surface appearances?

She knew she was being unreasonable. After all, her current assignment required her to convince people she was a hooker—and she was nothing if not an excellent actress. But no matter how unreasonable her reaction, Jake's acceptance hurt more than she could have imagined. After what had passed between them, how could he think it?

To keep from giving herself away, she schooled her features into a provocative smile. Levering herself up on one elbow, she reached over and slowly, seductively kissed him. "Could we talk later?" she asked, running her hand down his chest and over his firm stomach to the masculine part of him that had already begun to swell again. "At the moment there are a few more . . . stimulating things I'd rather do."

Admitting he was helpless against her sweet seduction, Jake groaned his capitulation.

Later . . . they'd talk later.

Pressed tightly against Jake's side, Alex fell into an exhausted sleep almost immediately after their last loving. But Jake was wide awake, his senses still too revved up by what had happened between them to sleep.

She lay so relaxed beside him. Almost . . . trusting. The thought left him feeling uncomfortable. He didn't want her trust. In the past he hadn't been very successful at taking care of those who'd given it to him.

Yet he had to admit there was something very gratifying about the fact that she'd shown him more trust than anyone in a long time.

She was the first woman who'd been able to make him lose control. He'd planned to show her another side to making love, one he'd thought she might not have experienced. But he'd ended up the student, learning things he'd never known existed. He'd been so wrapped up in her that he'd found himself a prisoner to his overpowering feelings for this woman.

He reminded himself, not for the first time, that he stayed away from situations that he might become emotionally involved in. He didn't want memories. They always came back in the darkest hours of the night to haunt him. Long ago he'd learned it was safer to substitute the adrenaline rush of taking down criminals for the much more personal danger of entrusting his heart to one woman. It was, he admitted, far from a perfect substitute, but protected the most vulnerable part of him.

He had an ironclad policy not to allow himself to fall in love. Not while his home was a virtual war zone—where the inhabitants didn't know from minute to minute when they might draw their last breath. Where whoever he cared for could be snatched from him in the beat of a heart... leaving pain and unbearable emptiness.

Alex shifted beside him, and he relished the feel of her naked body against his. His feelings for this woman ran deeper than he wanted to admit. But he'd always been brutally honest with himself, so he wouldn't back away from the truth now. He could get used to this—too damned easily.

He was overcome by a yearning so great that it terrified him. Why couldn't they have a life together? Because a family wasn't for him, the rational part of him admonished. He knew better than to wish for things that could never be his.

Still, watching Alex asleep beside him and remembering her spicy-sweet lovemaking, he allowed himself the luxury. They'd both been handed tough breaks in life and survived. They had that and a physical attraction hot enough to melt steel. It was more than a lot of couples he knew had going for them. Maybe, just maybe, fate would cut them some slack.

He drew Alex tighter against him and finally fell into a dreamless sleep.

The first streaks of dawn filtering through the small bedroom window pulled Alex from sleep. Jake's warm body was pressed spoon-fashion against her back, his arm draped over her waist, his hand cupping her breast. It felt so deliciously...right.

She eased from under his arm. Jake made a guttural sound of protest and rolled onto his back. Alex froze. When she was certain he wasn't going to awaken, she slipped gingerly from the bed.

For the space of several heartbeats, she allowed herself the luxury of absorbing the sight of Jake lying totally abandoned in sleep, one corner of the sheet just covering his groin. She felt her face flush. His dark hair was tousled from the countless times she'd shoved her hands into it to bring his mouth to hers, and his bare chest revealed faint marks that she must have put there during their uninhibited lovemaking.

This was the first time she'd seen him without his tautly honed defenses in place. She greedily absorbed all the memories and emotions coursing through her so that, after she'd gone, she could recall them in intimate detail.

Jake shifted slightly, and his brow puckered as if he were beginning to sense that all was not right. Alex drew in a quick breath. She had to leave before he woke and caught her sneaking away. The interlude was over. It was imperative that she get back to her world—and reality.

The longer she waited, the more she risked blowing her cover and endangering others. Not to mention her own vulnerable heart. The ache in her chest nearly overpowered her. She was leaving with Jake a part of herself that she'd never recover. Calling on her professional training, she silently gathered her things and tiptoed from the room.

In the kitchen she found a piece of paper and scrawled a brief note. Then, taking one last look around the shabby lodging that had served as safe harbor, she quietly left through the front door.

Jake knew Alex was gone even before he opened his eyes. Her comforting warmth, which she'd pressed against him throughout the early-morning hours, was absent. With his eyes still closed, he ran his hand over the side of the bed she'd occupied. The sheets were cold.

The small house had an empty, hollow feel to it, very similar to the emotion squeezing the region around his heart. He opened his eyes and sat up. Gauging the brightness of the light filtering through the bedroom window, he figured it to be midmorning, much later than he usually allowed himself to sleep. He swung his legs over the side of the mattress. It took a surprising amount of effort for him to reach for the jeans he'd discarded so eagerly mere hours before.

Reluctantly, he made his way to the kitchen. Wasn't that one of the first places a person looked for the inevitable desertion note? It didn't take him long to find it. As he'd suspected, she'd left it on the table.

He was startled to find that his hand shook as he picked up the slightly crinkled piece of paper. He'd tried to protect himself. He'd figured he could keep himself from becoming too emotionally involved. Unfortunately he'd figured wrong.

Forcing his eyes to the paper, he read.

Jake—
Your offer of help was touching, but I'm afraid I must decline. I have to be what I am. Thanks for everything. Take care.

Alex

Pain of the kind he hadn't experienced in years punched him in the gut. He crumpled the slip of paper into a tight ball and flung it across the room.

It figured, he thought cynically. For a brief time he'd recklessly let down his guard and trusted. The fact that she'd been able to walk out of his house without his even being aware of her leaving showed just how far she'd gotten past his defenses. He'd become so comfortable with her, felt so safe, that he'd slept the sleep of the dead. Or a fool.

Through sheer willpower he summoned anger to replace the pain, to keep him from identifying the emotion gnawing at him. How could he have been so stupid? He'd allowed her to disappear without finding out who she was or where she came from or what she knew. That fact put Sondra and her home at risk. But part of him rejected that possibility. Deep down he knew Alex wasn't a threat to any of them. At least not physically.

Hell, he was well rid of her, he rationalized. He certainly wasn't going to miss her. Why would he miss a woman who'd been trouble since she'd suddenly been thrust into his life? Who kept sticking her nose into areas he wanted left alone? He didn't need anyone like her around, challenging him, threatening that part of him that he'd guarded for so long.

He freely admitted he'd wanted her—still did, for that matter. But he'd been right in the first place. All he felt for Alex was pure and simple lust, intensified by the adrenaline high of being thrown together in a life-and-death situation.

Jake dragged a hand over his face, and a soft laugh escaped him. But the sound held no humor. No doubt that sex with Alex had been pure, but it sure as hell had been anything but simple. She'd left him with his emotions in turmoil, something he hadn't experienced since he'd watched his sister being lowered into the ground in the paupers' section of the local cemetery some twenty years ago.

Hell, who was he kidding? He already ached with missing Alex. And he'd already envisioned a half dozen scenarios of the kinds of trouble she could get into. In a corner of his mind he wanted desperately to ignore, he acknowledged that his feelings for Alex ran deep. Too deep.

Damn. What he needed right now was a good workout with one of the punching bags down at Mike's Gym.

The smell of stale sweat, ancient leather and the uniquely musty odor of old building greeted Jake as he entered Mike's Gym. Pungent smoke seemed to hang perpetually in the air, blurring the harsh ugliness of the bare brick walls. An empty boxing ring dominated one side of the large stuffy room.

The place felt comfortably familiar. This was his turf. It might not be pretty, but it was home. Over the years, he'd worked off a lot of frustration here.

It was too early for anyone else to be around. Old Mike was probably somewhere in the back, counting out the day's worth of threadbare towels. He knew there was nothing worth stealing up front.

Jake stripped out of his sweatshirt, jerked on a pair of padded gloves and, bare chested, headed for the nearest punching bag. With a determined thud, he lit into the unsuspecting bag, relishing the satisfying jolt all the way to his soul.

He landed each blow with one objective—to empty his mind. He didn't want to think. He didn't want to remember. The feel of Alex lying beside him in bed. The warmth of her under him, her silky tightness as he slid inside her . . .

He lost track of time. It was only him and the bag. Sweat trickled down his face and into his eyes, and his muscles began to protest.

Delivering another hard one-two jab, he caught sight of Will striding toward him.

"Where's Mary?" Will asked without preamble, worry furrowing his forehead. "I went by the house and she's not there."

"Gone." Jake gave the bag a punch that almost split its leather seams. "And her name's not Mary."

"What are you talking about, man?"

Breathing heavily, Jake grabbed the bag to stop its swaying. "I'm saying her name's not Mary. It's Alex." He watched comprehension spread across Will's face.

"She remembered?" he said, grinning. "Hey, that's great."

"Yeah, great." Jake gave the bag another blow, this time without quite as much enthusiasm. "You'll notice she didn't stick around."

Will's grin faded. "She's gone for good?"

Jake stepped away from the punching bag and grabbed a towel, wiping the sweat from his face and chest. "Looks like it." He didn't tell Will he harbored a tiny hope that she might show up, because the realistic part of him, the part that accepted as a given that life or fate or whatever it was that wouldn't cut him any slack, knew she wouldn't.

"Where'd she go?"

"She didn't bother to say."

"Aw, man!" A look of disbelief, quickly followed by frustrated disappointment, distorted Will's face. "She didn't say anything?"

Jake thought about her terse note. "Nothing important."

"Are you going after her?"

"No."

Will looked stunned. "Why not?"

Jake gave the bag one final resounding jab. "If she's interested, she knows where to find us."

"You can't mean that, Jake," he said accusingly. "She might need us. She could get into trouble."

The knot turning Jake's stomach inside out twisted a little tighter, but he tried to ignore the fact that he had the same fear. "Forget her, Will," he said, heading for the showers. "That's what I'm doing."

Forget her, hell. Jake stepped into the chipped ceramic shower stall and turned on the cold water full force. Letting the icy spray beat down on him, he conceded he was lying to Will. To himself. He wasn't going to be able to forget Alex whatever-her-last-name-was for a long, long time. Maybe never.

But the chill didn't drive away the worry. He kept remembering Debbie, imagining what it would have been like for her, being totally alone, running from God knew what. That had to be the reason he was so concerned about Alex, he told himself.

He turned off the water and stepped out of the ancient stall. Picking up a towel, he began drying himself. Somehow Jake knew his concern for her would eventually force him to track her down, make sure she was okay.

That thought scared the hell out of him.

Chapter Eleven

Alex fingered the intricate design on the thick comforter covering her king-size bed. She let her gaze wonder around the opulent room that had begun to feel more like a prison than the room she'd slept in most of her life. This house had never been one of her favorite places to begin with. Now it was becoming unbearable. "I don't understand why everyone's making such a fuss," Alex grumbled to Stephanie.

Stephanie eyed her younger sister, her expression holding concern tinged with tolerant humor. "The fact that you gashed your head open, were knocked unconscious, lost your memory and disappeared for several days might have something to do with it," she replied dryly.

"It wasn't that big a deal." Alex spoke matter-of-factly, as if stating it would make it so.

"Dr. Simmons said whoever put in your stitches did an excellent job. You probably won't have much of a scar."

Alex waved her comment aside. "I'm not worried about a scar." There was no doubt that Sondra Harding had known what she was doing. Alex touched the tiny ridge of skin that would forever be a reminder of the man who'd inadvertently given it to her. She felt the protective casing she'd painstakingly erected around her heart shift precariously. "You see? I'm fine." Throwing back the covers, she began climbing out of bed.

In resignation, Stephanie grabbed a bathrobe and tossed it to Alex. "I think you're rushing things, sis. You've only been back a few days, and Dr. Simmons said you should take it easy."

"That's all I've done. For days." Alex slipped on the satin robe and belted it, then, hands on hips, turned to face her sister. "If I have to stay cooped up in this house or lie in that bed one more hour, I'm going to start climbing walls."

Of course, a little voice taunted, *if Jake McAlister were in bed with you, you wouldn't feel that way.* Alex clamped down hard on the wayward thought. She had to stop thinking like that, she told herself firmly. Jake McAlister was past history.

"Why don't you enjoy the vacation? It's the first one you've had in years. Even your boss ordered you to take some time off."

Alex hugged her arms across her waist and paced to the window. "In case everyone's forgotten, I'm still on assignment."

"How can anyone forget? Police work is your whole life." Stephanie sighed. "I wish you'd give it up. It's too dangerous, and you have a nasty tendency of taking too many risks.''

More than her sister could possibly imagine, Alex reflected, thinking of the risk to her heart. "Only when it's absolutely necessary," she defended herself, trying to sooth Stephanie's fears before she began to lecture in earnest.

"Lie to yourself if you have to," Stephanie said, speaking in the too-quiet tone that signaled anyone who knew her that she was deadly serious. "But don't lie to me. I know you too well. There's little you won't try in your misguided quest to prove your worth to the world."

Alex glanced over her shoulder at her sister. "You know how important my work is to me." But even as she made the assertion, she realized that after the past few days, her reasons for entering police work no longer seemed quite so compelling. The realization made her uneasy. She rubbed her arms. Police work had been a major part of her life for a long time.

"I understand why you think it is." Stephanie's expression softened. "But it can't give you much comfort if you're dead."

"Seems lately everyone's interested in giving me career advice," Alex muttered darkly.

"Sorry." Stephanie sent her sister a speculative look. "Has someone else been trying to talk sense to you?"

Did she want to discuss this, Alex wondered, even with Stephanie? She stared out at the perfectly manicured grounds of her childhood home. Was she ready?

"You haven't said much about what happened while you were away from us," Stephanie persisted when Alex didn't respond.

Alex heard the implicit question. Leaving her post by the window, she began pacing around the room. "There isn't much to tell." Unless you count becoming emotionally involved with a man concealing a suspicious background—or at the very least a mysterious one. A man who, for some inexplicable reason, Alex felt compelled to protect.

Because it was expected of a cop coming off an assignment, Alex had been debriefed and had given Bob Griffin, her superior and friend, a full report. It was written in the customary, objective, just-the-facts-ma'am police jargon. She'd deliberately glossed over the parts that might incriminate Jake. After all, she'd rationalized, the man had put his life on the line for her. She owed him. She couldn't bring herself to turn him in.

She'd also prudently omitted the intimate nature of their time together. As well as the emotional upheaval those few days had cost her—would continue to cost her—for God knew how long.

She intended to discreetly uncover as much information as she could about the man who'd shaken the foundation of her emotionally safe existence. The Jake McAlister she'd gotten to know simply couldn't be what he appeared. She couldn't reconcile a drug dealer helping a kid from the streets. Or helping a minister.

Besides, he'd risked his life to save hers and, however misguided, had offered to help her find another "profession." No matter what she discovered about him, no matter who he was, she owed him and she'd find a way to help him.

But the nagging question remained: Could her faith in him be faulty?

"What's got you so uptight, sis?" Stephanie prompted softly.

Alex stopped pacing and shoved her hands into the pockets of her robe. "Do you remember a man named George Brady?"

Stephanie considered the question for several seconds, and Alex could almost see her sister's photographic memory sorting for answers. "Grandfatherly type in a Hollywood kinda way. Good connections, but no visible means of support. Usually included on Mother and Father's guest list for certain social functions."

"That's the one. What's your impression of him?"

Stephanie shrugged. "I remember him being a pleasant enough guy. Why?"

"Did you find anything . . . odd about him?"

"I wouldn't say he was one of my favorite people, but he seemed okay." Stephanie looked at her sister questioningly. "Then again, it's been a while since I last saw him. In fact, I don't think I've spoken to him more than a few times since Mother and Father died. What are you getting at, sis?"

Alex shook her head and rubbed her arms, suddenly realizing she was probably saying too much. She knew better than to discuss details of an ongoing case with someone outside the department, even Stephanie. And it looked as if George Brady was an integral part of this case. "Oh, nothing important," she prevaricated. "I ran into him again recently. Just wanted your opinion."

Somewhere along the line, Alex's instincts had failed her regarding George Brady. Discovering that the longtime family acquaintance could be mixed up in drug dealings had come as a shock. Although she'd never particularly liked the guy, she'd known Brady for years. Yet even with all her police training, she'd never suspected him of being dirty. It shook her confidence in her ability to judge human nature. Should she trust her instincts when it came to Jake McAlister?

Stephanie looked at Alex as if the blow to her head might have caused more damage than first suspected. "What has all this got to do with your resting for a few days?"

"Not a thing," Alex said dismissively, then changed the subject. "I've been home the better part of a week, and I still don't have a report on McAlister."

"The guy who helped you while you were in trouble?" Stephanie asked, still watching her sister closely.

"Yeah." Alex had given her a thumbnail sketch of what happened while she'd been missing. Just enough to ease her sister's mind, but without specific details.

"Maybe Nick can help. After all, he does have a knack for locating hard-to-find people."

That brought a smile to Alex's face. "And very cleverly, as I recall," she said, remembering how resourceful her brother-in-law, a government operative, had been in tracking down the seven-year-old son he hadn't known existed and the boy's mother— who just happened to be Stephanie. "As a matter of fact, I've already asked him to see what he can find out through his sources."

"Well, then, with that off your mind, you should be able to relax."

"Wrong, Steph." Alex headed for the cavernous walk-in closet on the other side of the room. "I'm going down to the precinct." Something told her she should check on the status of this case.

"Bob told you specifically not to worry about work. In fact, he ordered you not to show your face for a week."

"Close enough." Alex disappeared into the depths of the closet. "Besides," she added, her voice sounding muffled, "it won't hurt to light a few fires under a few select tushes."

A couple of hours later, Alex breezed into the squad room and headed straight for Bob Griffin's office. Because her intuition told her she might be in for a fight, she'd chosen to wear one of her "power suits." She'd pulled her hair into a French braid, applied understated makeup and finished off with a pair of chic pumps. No one had to tell her that the effect was stunning. But she hadn't dressed this way because it made her look beautiful. She used it as armor, to make herself appear formidable.

"Hi, Tracy," she said, when she reached the young woman sitting at the desk strategically positioned outside Bob's door. "Is he in?"

"He's in," Tracy confirmed, "but I'm not sure you'll like what you find."

Alex laughed. "Trouble?"

Tracy rolled her eyes. "Isn't there always?" She picked up the phone, spoke into it briefly, then motioned Alex toward the closed door. "He's all yours. Good luck."

"Thanks." Alex stepped around the desk and tapped a light tattoo on the deputy chief's door.

"Come in." Bob Griffin's curt tone did not bode well for an amicable meeting.

Taking a deep breath, she opened the door.

"What the hell are you doing here?" Bob barked before she'd fully crossed the threshold.

"And hello to you, too," she said sweetly, deciding to try for flippancy. "What can I say? You're my addiction, and I needed a fix."

"Yeah, right," he groused, a brief boyish grin transforming his hard features. "I told you I didn't want to see your beautiful face for at least a week."

"And it's been a week. Almost." Alex strolled over to the vacant chair directly across the desk from him. "Besides, there's nothing wrong with me. I was fine a week ago and I'm fine now." *Liar, liar,* a tiny part of her taunted.

Bob leaned back in his big swivel chair. "Actually, I'm glad you're here. Saves me having to send for you."

"That's a little hard to believe, considering the reception I just received." As she started to take her seat, a movement in the chair located to the right of Bob's desk caught her attention. The chair was large and overstuffed and, with its back to the door, easily concealed whoever sat there—particularly if the person slouched in it. Even in profile, she had no trouble recognizing the chair's occupant.

Jake McAlister!

Shock, and something unidentifiable, reverberated through Alex, but training and self-control came to her rescue. She settled into her chair as if finding her former lover in her boss's office was an everyday occurrence. Jake was dressed in the same grungy clothing he'd worn the first night she'd seen him. Had he been arrested? Was that why Bob had been about to send for her?

Without blinking, Alex forced her attention back to Bob and waited.

He leaned forward and propped his elbows on the desk. "I want you to turn over all the files on your current case."

Confusion added itself to the other emotions fluttering around inside her. "Why?"

"Because you're being taken off the case."

Dumbfounded, all she could do was stare. "Excuse me?" she said, certain she'd misunderstood.

"You're off the case," he repeated warily.

"Why?" This time it was a demand.

Bob cleared his throat, flicked his gaze to Jake, then back to her. "Because you've done enough. After what you've been through, you deserve some time off."

"That's bull, and you know it." Alex allowed herself a quick glance at Jake. He hadn't so much as looked at her since she'd entered the room. She returned her attention to the boss who'd been her friend nearly as long as she'd been on the force. "You can't do this, Bob. I've spent weeks collecting information essential to this case."

"Any information you have should be in the file. It'll be passed on to the...uh...person taking over."

Again Alex glanced at Jake. He sat relaxed, his right booted foot crossed over his left jeans-clad knee. But now his ice-blue eyes were trained on her, his face expressionless. The impact of his direct stare sent an electric shock through her. "Should we be discussing this in front of him?" she asked Bob.

"Sorry," Bob said. He shifted restlessly in his chair. "Alex this is Lt. Jake McAlister. Jake, meet Detective Alex Harcourt."

Jake McAlister was a cop? Alex schooled her features not to betray her. What was she supposed to do now? Alex wondered frantically, sorting through her options. She could pretend they'd never met. Or she could casually say, We've already had the pleasure. In fact, we know each other intimately. Better yet, she could tell them both to go to hell. Prudently, she said nothing and waited for the other shoe to drop.

"He's been assigned to take over the case," Bob said conversationally, saving her from making a fool of herself.

"I don't think I understand," she said carefully.

Jake continued to watch her through dispassionate eyes. "It's really quite simple." He spoke for the first time since she'd entered the room, his voice low, controlled. "The case is mine."

Alex struggled to assimilate everything. This was not the man she'd gotten to know such a short while ago. The man she'd made love with throughout one soul-shattering night. The man whose body she knew intimately and who intimately knew hers.

This man was a stranger—a stranger coldly determined to have his way. She would not stoop to arguing when it was obvious the decision was already made. Instead, she chose anger as her shield. She rose gracefully to her feet and straightened her shoulders. "Since I have information pertinent to *your* case," she said, thinking of her connection with George Brady, "you might find me of some assistance."

Jake slowly unfolded from the chair and stood, his gaze searing her. "If you're referring to George Brady and the fact that you know him, I'm aware of it."

Why wasn't she surprised he already had that information? she wondered. Now Jake had one more thing to hold against her. Once again someone from her world, an outsider, was wreaking havoc in his.

"I don't work with a partner," he stated succinctly.

"Any partner—" she crossed her arms protectively at her waist "—or just me?"

One side of his mouth lifted in the semblance of a smile. "You have to admit, your past performance didn't cover you with glory."

Alex felt her face flame and had to concede, albeit grudgingly, that he had a point. She'd screwed up big time that night, putting him as well as herself in danger.

"If it's any consolation," he said, softening marginally, "it's not just you. I don't work with any cop from any police department."

Refusing to be placated, she took a moment to digest that. "What do you have against other cops?"

His stance suggested it wouldn't be smart to challenge him. "Most of them are outsiders. They don't have a clue how to handle the problems plaguing my part of town. Ultimately they're more hindrance than help."

"Interesting concept," Alex commented. "And how do you propose to take care of the criminal element in your part of town?"

"With resident cops who understand the people who live there. Train our own to protect our own."

Alex felt the rebuff of Jake's us-versus-them phi-
losophy like a slap in the face. She looked at Bob be-
seechingly. "Dammit, Bob, this is my case. I have a
right to see it through to the end."

Bob had the good sense to look chagrined. "We
don't have a choice."

"You know my knowledge of this case could be vital," she reiterated.

"Put it in the file," Bob told her flatly. "You heard
McAlister. He won't work with you."

She refused to look at Jake. "Does he have final
say?"

"In this instance, yes."

"Why?" She was beginning to feel like a parrot.

"Because his part in this investigation is more critical than yours."

"And bottom line," Jake told Alex, "I work
alone." His gaze burned into her. Then he trans-
ferred his attention to Bob Griffin. "I will not take
responsibility for keeping her out of trouble. I'll leave
it to you to work out the details." He turned on his
heel and walked out.

There was a subtle finality about the soft sound of
the door closing behind him.

She stared at the door for several seconds. "How
can he do this?"

"I'm sorry, Alex. The department tried to work
this out with McAlister, but he flatly refused to co-
operate. He's not regular police. He's with a special
independent task force, and what you stumbled into
is an operation he's been working on for several
months. He feels...strongly about it." Bob grimaced and shrugged helplessly. "It's his baby, so it's
his call."

"I guess I'll have to learn to live with it, then, won't I? But I don't have to like it." While she understood how important this case was to Jake, she resented his arrogance. But most of all, his careless dismissal of her hurt far more than she could have anticipated.

She'd deliberately chosen the macho environment of police work to prove her worth beyond her surface beauty. It also served as an element of control she'd badly needed after surviving a mugging years ago. She'd worked long and hard to gain respect and earn her position within the department. She competed in a man's world—and now a man, a man who seemed determined to mistake her for something she wasn't, was trying to steal it from her.

Worse, she very much feared she was falling in love with the man in question.

Jake McAlister was a cop. She let the knowledge sink in. Here she'd been worried about him, trying to find a way to protect him, only to discover he was a damned cop!

In three strides she was out the door after him.

"Wait just a damned minute, McAlister."

Jake stopped in resignation and turned to watch Alexandra Harcourt hurry down the hall to catch up with him. He'd read the stats on her. Seeing her in her designer suit rather than sweats or a sexy pair of shorts brought it home. She looked classy and elegant. And way out of his league. He knew it and it made him mad—mad enough to want to strike out. To hurt her as she'd hurt him. To push her away before she could do any more damage to his shaky defenses.

He recalled how he'd thought about trying to redeem Alex, to save her from herself where he hadn't been able to save his sister. The thought added to his sense of betrayal. Damn, but he was a first-class fool.

"How dare you!" Alex snapped when she reached him.

Jake didn't want to notice her slightly flushed face. Or the rapid rise and fall of her chest as she fought to catch her breath. Or the way her eyes sparkled with anger. Or the way the suit molded her figure, reminding him of what lay under it. He knew those curves. Intimately. He slid his hands into the back pockets of his jeans to keep from sliding them into her hair and destroying its perfection.

He raised an eyebrow. "How dare I what?" he asked in what he hoped was a casual tone.

"Have me taken off this case! I can help you."

Several people jostled by them, and he steered Alex to one side of the crowded hallway. "Like the way you helped nearly get us both killed?" To his surprise, the flash of remorse in her eyes gave him no pleasure, but he refused to let it stop him. For the sake of his sanity and, more important, her safety, he had to get her out of his life. "If I hadn't seen your records, I'd wonder how the hell you passed training."

She looked momentarily nonplussed, then quickly recovered. He admired her for that. "Of course. You had me investigated." She crossed her arms. "Let me guess—you ran my fingerprints."

He didn't bother to confirm it. He knew she was as familiar with the procedure as he was. "I like to know who I'm dealing with. Learning about you was very...enlightening."

"Really?" she said, her tone mocking.

Jake spotted a group of women, three abreast, approaching fast. "Let's get out of this traffic," he muttered. Grabbing her arm, he headed down the hall to find an unoccupied conference room. He wanted this matter settled between them so he could get Alex Harcourt out of his hair once and for all. Now was as good a time as any.

It hadn't taken him long after Alex's disappearance to realize that for his peace of mind—not to mention his heart, he'd have to locate the elusive woman who'd made an emotional shambles of his life. Learning she was a cop had made him angry, but the anger had been tempered with understanding. He knew the importance of a cop protecting her cover. Hell, he'd done the same thing.

Yet discovering that she'd perpetuated the lie that she was a prostitute had knocked him for a loop. The logical part of him might understand. But a deeper emotional part—the part he'd protected for so long—wasn't interested in logic. How could she have shared something so beautiful with him and not have been honest about this? How could he trust her? How could he trust *himself* with her?

Once he'd read the report on her and realized just how high up the social ladder she was, he'd figured she'd gotten a kick out of making love with someone from the dark side of society. Pain slashed at him, making it difficult to breathe. They hadn't made love, he reminded himself harshly, they'd had sex. Lust, fueled by the adrenaline rush of a life-and-death situation. He had to remember that.

She'd had her fun, then run back to her world. Why would someone like Alex Harcourt be interested in a relationship with someone like him? No way in hell would she want to become a permanent part of his life. He'd been a fool to even entertain the idea.

When their separate departments had suggested he and Alex team up on this case, Jake had flatly refused. No way in hell could he handle working with her on a daily basis.

But beyond that, he had too damned much difficulty maintaining his objectivity when he was close to her. That was dangerous—for her and for him. He knew her record. She deliberately volunteered for cases that were on the edge. She took too many chances. And though he hated admitting it, the possibility that he might not be able to keep her out of harm's way tied his gut in knots.

Finally finding an empty room at the far end of the hall, he ushered Alex inside and closed the door behind them.

Alex shook off his hold on her arm the moment they were inside. "You were saying?" she prompted. Her chin came up as if she were bracing for a fight.

Good, he thought, he was ready to give her one. "What the hell are you doing in police work? Did you get tired of the good life and decide slumming might be an interesting change of pace?"

For a moment, shock was plain on her face before she concealed it. She moved to the other side of the room. "I'm always up for a new adventure," she said flippantly, folding her arms. "But I'm not certain I understand what you're getting at."

Her defiance got to him. It had from the first. It made her appear vulnerable, as if she were taking on the whole world all alone. "Go back to your ivory tower, Helen of Troy," he told her softly. "This isn't your fight. You don't belong in my world."

"What's your point?"

"What I do isn't a game to me, Detective Harcourt. I'm not doing this until something more exciting comes along."

He'd gone into police work as a release, as a means of healing after Debbie's senseless death. He guessed that a shrink would probably say he was trying to ease his pain by trying to fix the world. But Jake knew it wasn't anything that grand. His work was his reality. It had started in desperation as vengeance after his sister's death but over time had become his salvation. Admittedly, it made for a bleak existence, but he'd accepted that.

Until Alex Harcourt had exploded into his life, making him question himself. His anger returned.

She squared her shoulders, holding herself ramrod straight. "Are you suggesting that I'm not serious about my work?"

Jake hesitated a beat. "What I'm saying is you have no reason to take on this fight. Unlike your world, mine is a struggle just to stay alive. In mine you have to fight to keep what's yours, including your life." And he didn't like to even think about Alex fighting for hers.

Alex's direct gaze didn't falter. "You don't have a monopoly on crime," she said quietly. "And I'll put my training up against yours any time you want. I'm more than qualified to work with you on this case."

"I can't work with someone I don't trust," he told her curtly. "You weren't honest with me."

He saw her flinch, but she didn't pretend to misunderstand. "What was I supposed to do? Tell you who I really was?"

"That would have been a start."

"I couldn't blow my cover," Alex reminded Jake. "Any more than you could." But that little voice kept whispering to her that she was lying—to him, to herself.

"Maybe you couldn't tell me you were a cop on assignment," he conceded, watching her with ice-cold eyes. "But you sure as hell could have told me you weren't a hooker."

Suddenly realizing the trap she'd laid for herself, Alex offered no rebuttal. She couldn't tell him the truth. That after what he'd told her about himself, his past, she'd figured he'd think better of her if he believed she was a common hooker rather than from the upper level of society. An admission like that would reveal just how important his opinion of her had become to her. And self-preservation told her that would not be wise.

"You're good, I'll give you that," he finally said when she remained silent. "Did you get some perverted pleasure in playing the ignorant guy from the slums for a fool?"

"I can vouch for the fact that you're anything but ignorant," she retorted. "But the fool part is another issue entirely."

"Why did you let me make love to you?"

Alex sucked in a sharp breath. She hadn't expected him to broach that subject. "Why not?" she said, choosing her words for retaliation to hold him at bay. "It seemed logical. I wanted you, you wanted me."

"And that's all it meant? Just hot sex."

Pain squeezed her chest, but she wouldn't allow her gaze to waver. She would come out of this fray with her pride intact, even if her heart was bleeding. She would not let him know just how badly he'd hurt her. "That describes it, I believe. What more could it be?"

Jake felt the bite of her words to his soul. "Isn't it time you moved on to another line of work?" He didn't want to believe she was simply a rich girl playing at being a cop, but she wasn't refuting it. Maybe if he made himself believe she was superficial, he could convince himself he really didn't give a damn about her, or her safety.

"What makes you think I'm tired of police work?"

He shrugged negligently. "According to your file, you've had quite a variety of careers—from socialite to model. I figured by now you'd be bored with this one." He knew he was being a bastard, but he had to feed his animosity. That or drag her into his arms and see if she felt and tasted as good as he remembered.

Alex almost staggered under the whip of his cynicism. She hadn't expected his opinion of her to matter so much. Drawing on all her composure, she walked to the door. Pausing, she looked back at him.

"You're right, Jake. It's time to move on." She refused to defend herself. She would not leave herself open to any more of his careless rejection. She would not tell him her reasons for joining the police force. She would not tell him about the brutal attack that had changed her life.

"Fine," he said. "You have nothing to offer my world. I don't want or need your help."

"Looks like we both get what we want. Me off the case. I wish you luck in apprehending the scum." She held his gaze a second longer. "Keep...well."

This time it was her turn to leave the room, closing the door with ominous softness behind her.

Chapter Twelve

By the time she reached her Mercedes, Alex was shaking so badly that she had trouble inserting the key into the ignition. Finally she gave up trying and leaned her head against the back of the seat. Taking a deep breath, she waited for the pain to kick in.

She had to force herself to think about something else or the memory of Jake's terse words would cut her to ribbons. She focused on Will and Sondra and Nathan. The past several years of Alex's life had been taken up with trying to make a difference. She wanted to help. She *needed* to help. And by damn, she *did* have something to offer. At least in one particular case.

Several days later, Alex stood outside the church rectory and tapped on Nathan Garner's office door.

"Well, this is a pleasant surprise," Nathan said, opening the door and ushering her into the small room that looked out on the garden. "It's been a while. Are you well?"

"Fine, thanks."

He studied her for a moment. "So, other than your health, how are things?"

Alex glanced out at the tranquil outdoor scene, trying not to remember what had transpired between her and Jake the last time she'd been in the small rectory garden. She pulled her gaze back to Nathan. "They could be better."

He nodded sympathetically. "So I gathered from Jake's rather disagreeable disposition recently."

She seated herself in the chair Nathan offered. "Then you understand why I haven't been around."

"I understand that Jake is being his usual... charming self."

Alex's laugh held little humor. "You could say that. Jake made it clear he doesn't want me interfering in 'his world,' as he puts it."

"Well, remember this, Alex. No matter what Jake says, you're always welcome here."

"Thank you." The warmth of Nathan's reception helped ease the ache that had been growing inside her for days. "I suppose Jake gave you his version of my life history."

Nathan smiled crookedly, and Alex was again struck by how unlikely a candidate he was for the role of a minister. "Only a few pertinent facts. Your name, for example. And that your profession is—shall we say—on the right side of the law."

"Well, at least he didn't bore you," Alex said wryly.

"I got the impression there's a lot more going on than his terse summary indicated."

Alex shifted in her chair.

"Sorry. I have a bad habit of prying. Forget I said anything." He flashed his killer smile again. "What can I do for you?"

Relieved that he wasn't going to press, she returned his smile. "The reason I'm here is to offer my help."

"Considering the encouragement you've received from some sources, that's generous of you. But you'll find that I, unlike Jake, greedily take all offers." The amusement left him, and she again glimpsed that puzzling sadness. "There's so much to do here. Too much."

She rummaged in her purse, withdrew a pen and her checkbook and quickly filled out a check. "There's one stipulation," she said, adding her distinctive signature. "I don't want my name spread around. Please keep this between the two of us."

"If that's what you want."

"It is." Alex rose and handed him the check.

Nathan looked at the piece of paper, then back at her, amazement clearly visible on his face. "I think you put in at least a couple of zeros too many. This is more than generous, Alex."

Alex felt embarrassment warm her face. "What you're doing here is worth much more than this. And I want to help." She shrugged. "This is one way I can without . . . upsetting Jake."

"We'll put it to good use. It'll go a long way toward funding several projects. I guess I don't have to tell you how much I—all of us—appreciate this."

"What you're doing is so important, so vital. I wish . . ." Alex let her words trail away, then glanced at her watch. "Well, I have to run. It's good to see you again, Nathan."

He came around the desk and draped an arm around her shoulders. "Thanks for coming by." He gestured toward the check lying on the desk. "And I'm not referring to your generosity."

"Thank you and you're welcome. Oh." She pulled a card from her purse and handed it to him. "I'm worried about Will. And Cilla's problem and how it's affecting him. If you ever need anything, anything at all, please contact me."

"I notice you didn't mention Jake's name." Nathan gave her a brotherly hug. "Don't give up on him."

"I'm afraid it's the other way around," Alex said, having difficulty speaking around the tightness in her throat. "He's given up on me."

"My offer still holds. Anytime you want to talk, I'm available. Jake may be a fool, but I'm not." He smiled wryly. "At least that's what I try to convince myself."

"Thanks again." Alex leaned up and kissed him on the cheek. "You're a good man, Nathan Garner. Take care of yourself."

On her way out of the church, Alex rounded a corner and almost collided with a woman heading in the opposite direction. Reaching out to steady the other woman, Alex stepped back to apologize.

"Sorry," she said, "I wasn't looking . . . Sondra!"

"Well, well, well. Look who's here." Sondra gave Alex a quick appraisal. "How're you doing?"

"I'm fine." Alex thought she detected just a hint of reserve in Sondra's tone. "You'll be happy to learn that my doctor seems to think your surgical technique is quite remarkable."

Some of the aloofness left the older woman's face. "No permanent damage, huh?"

Alex shook her head. "In fact, Dr. Simmons says I probably won't have a scar." She hesitated. "Since I left in a bit of a hurry the other day, I didn't get a chance to properly thank you for what you did for me. I did . . . do appreciate it."

"No problem," Sondra said, brushing aside her gratitude. "We have an understanding, Jake and me. He asks and I try to deliver."

Alex chuckled and glanced down the gloomy hallway toward the doorway leading outside. Bright autumn sunlight filtered through the dingy glass panels. "Is there somewhere close by we can get a cup of tea or coffee?"

"I have a better suggestion. Why don't we try the church kitchen? Nathan keeps a good supply of both on hand."

"You're right," Alex said, recalling the spiced tea Nathan had made for her that served as the trigger to her memory. "Lead the way." With mixed emotions, she couldn't help wondering what would have happened if she still had amnesia.

Once they'd made pots of both tea and coffee, Alex and Sondra sat at the beat-up kitchen counter, sipping their drinks in companionable silence.

Alex set down her mug. "I guess Jake told you why I left in such a hurry."

"Jake doesn't do much talking. But he said enough to give me a pretty good idea of what happened."

Then Sondra knew more than she did, Alex thought with irony, because she was still trying to make sense of what had happened between her and Jake. She couldn't help envying Jake and Sondra's relationship. They seemed to understand each other. Alex had wondered often what kind of woman appealed to Jake McAlister. It certainly didn't appear to be anyone like herself. He was such a self-contained man, she'd learned during her short time with him, that she doubted he'd appreciate the clinging type. Which was more or less what she'd been reduced to while she'd been his . . . guest.

"How long have you known Jake?" she asked Sondra.

She seemed to consider the question carefully for a moment, then, as if reaching some conclusion, said, "I've known Jake since he was a kid. His sister, Debbie, and I went back a long way."

"You must miss her very much."

Sondra looked surprised. "Jake told you about Debbie?"

Alex took a sip of her tea, then held the mug with both hands. "Some," she hedged, wondering how much she should reveal to this woman.

"That's unusual. He never talks about Debbie."

"He didn't give many details, but what he did say sounded pretty bleak."

"Debbie and I went through hell together." Deep sorrow flickered in Sondra's eyes. "I made it. She didn't."

"That had to have been rough on both you and Jake."

"It was. It left Jake totally alone at a time when a kid needs all the help he can get. I was still messed up with drugs, so I was less than worthless. In fact, Jake took care of me. If it hadn't been for him, I would've ended up just like Debbie."

And that explained, thought Alex, why Sondra was so accommodating to Jake. She felt he'd saved her life. The image of Jake forced to take on the responsibilities of a man before having the opportunity simply to be a child left Alex feeling raw inside. Sensing Sondra's profound guilt, she searched for something to ease the tension. "Obviously you figured out how to make up for lost time. Must be why he seems to take it for granted that he can impose on your generosity anytime he wants."

The older woman laughed, softening the lines left on her face by years of hard living. "Maybe. But he knows his work's important to me, too. It was Debbie's death that drove him to work with the law. I think he thought of it as a form of legal vengeance." Her smile deepened. "Of course at times he tends to push the boundaries of what's legal."

Alex chuckled and shook her head. "Under the right circumstances, I don't doubt it."

"He never asks for help."

"I've noticed. But I don't understand why."

Sondra took her time replying. "He considers it a sign of weakness."

"But at one time or another, all of us need help."

"Not Jake. He'll do it on his own or die in the attempt."

"That makes for a very lonely, not to mention dangerous, existence." Alex moved her mug around, forming concentric rings of moisture on the countertop. "He asks for your help," she commented quietly, feeling an inexplicable pinch of envy.

"Yes, he does," Sondra agreed. "But I've proved to him I can take care of myself. And he's learned over the years that he can trust me." She finished off her coffee, then carefully set her mug on the counter. "You have to understand. Jake doesn't want to be responsible for anyone but himself."

"But why?" Alex asked, surprised.

"Because ever since Debbie's death, he's afraid he might fail them."

"You're a very astute woman, Sondra Harding," Alex told her, sensing there was more being said than what she was hearing. "Why are you still stuck in this part of town? Why haven't you used your talents to get away from here—" her gesture encompassed the shabby surroundings, both inside and out "—and leave all this behind?"

Sondra shrugged. "It's my home. I grew up in this neighborhood."

"But doesn't it hold bad memories? Or worse, strong temptations?"

"Yes." A sad smile came and went on Sondra's face. "But memories are always with you, and temptation is everywhere. You can't run from it. It'll always find you. The trick," she said, pouring herself another mug of coffee, "is learning to be stronger than it is.

"Besides," she continued, "I understand what folks who live here have to deal with every day." She shrugged. "Because I understand, I have no choice but to help."

On a flash of insight, Alex suddenly comprehended what drove Jake. What held him here. He thought of this as a challenge. He had to prove he was stronger than all the temptations and dangers. Alex understood about having to prove yourself. But Jake went even further. He believed he had to fix the things that had caused him, and those he cared for, so much hurt.

The revelation left Alex shaken. The contrast between his life and hers was staggering.

Jake sprawled on the old sofa in the row house, cradling a can of lukewarm soda in his hands. He took a swig and grimaced. What he really wanted was a bottle of Scotch. And no glass. Anything that would block out the images of Alex that kept haunting his thoughts.

He couldn't remember the last time he'd had the desire to get drunk. But he couldn't do it here. Liquor, or any drug for that matter, was absolutely forbidden in Sondra's house. Besides, he simply didn't have the energy, or the motivation, to find somewhere else to court oblivion and a raging hangover.

He set down the can of soda. It certainly wasn't going to do the job. But then he had serious doubts anything would. He had what he wanted: Alex off the case and out of his life.

So why the hell did he feel so lousy?

Laying his head against the back of the sofa, he closed his eyes and waited for the vision of Alex to fill his mind's eye. The last time he'd seen her, she'd looked so damned sexy in her designer suit. And so untouchable. He'd wanted to strip it off her and wrestle her to the floor. He'd wanted to reignite the intimate, abandoned look she'd had when they'd made love, just before he'd pushed her over the edge of her first climax. He felt his body respond to the image, and he muttered a curse.

He should be thinking about his investigation. He sat up and grabbed the police folder off the small table next to him and forced himself to open it. The gang who'd been peddling drugs in this area had to have a supplier outside the neighborhood. He'd devoted the better part of a year planning how he was going to bring him down. Now, thanks to Alex's detailed report, he knew how to find the likely suspect. George Brady. That's what he should be concentrating on. Not this wrenching longing for Alex Harcourt.

But the sense of gratification, the sense of reward usually present when he was about to bring in a criminal, was absent. Instead of the usual high, he felt hollow inside.

Guilt ate at him. He tossed the folder aside. Jake wondered if he'd ever erase the memory of the way she'd looked as she walked out the door of that police conference room, a cold veneer protecting her.

He knew how he'd feel if he was in her position. No way in hell would he sit still for being pulled off a case. But Alex was different, he tried to convince himself.

She'd moved up through the police ranks at the speed of light. She'd pulled strings, using her considerable influence—influence unavailable to the average cop—to get what she wanted. As far as he could tell, she was in it for the thrill of living on the edge. She hadn't paid the price in blood, sweat and tears to reach her present position. How serious could she be?

To his way of thinking, there were too many similarities between Alex and Barbara. Barbara had been a socialite, a country club do-gooder, who used her influence to get what she wanted, to manipulate others. She'd interfered in Debbie's life. But when confronted with a problem she didn't want to be bothered with, Barbara had disappeared. Ultimately, her casual attitude had destroyed Debbie.

He figured Alex had wanted a taste of how the other half lived. Slumming, he called it. She'd had her fun. Now it was time for her to move on to something more appropriate for a woman from her level of society. Alex would've eventually grown tired of her latest game of charades and gone back to her world. By having her pulled off the case, he silently argued, he'd simply speeded up the process.

But even as he tried to convince himself otherwise, in the deepest part of him, Jake knew the real reason he wanted her off the case had nothing to do with how serious she might or might not be. And had everything to do with his dread that she was going to get hurt. Or worse. Plain and simple, she'd gotten past his defenses. He'd come to care for her far more than was wise.

And he was gut-level scared that he wouldn't be able to protect her.

What he needed was a distraction. As if on cue, the sound of impatient footsteps on the porch supplied it. A moment later, the front door banged open to admit Will.

When he spotted Jake, relief spread across his face. "Cool," he said, "you're here."

A half smile lifted Jake's mouth, and he nodded. "Looks like it."

Having established the obvious, Will stuffed his hands in his pockets and reverted to his usual taciturn manner. He prowled the room.

Jake waited. He knew it wouldn't do any good to rush the kid. He'd talk when he was ready.

Finally Will stopped pacing. "You heard anything from Mary... I mean, Alex?"

The question surprised Jake. Teenagers rarely paid much attention to adults, and one who'd passed through Will's life as rapidly as Alex had shouldn't have made much of an impression. Who was he kidding? Jake silently chided. She'd certainly made one hell of an impression on *him*.

"Why?" Jake hedged. He'd feel a lot better if Will wasn't quite so intrigued with Alex. He was setting himself up for a fall. Why should she give a damn about the problems confronting a boy from the slums? She had nothing in common with them, couldn't possibly understand their world.

"I dunno." In typical teenage fashion, now that Will had his attention, he was reluctant to come right out and tell Jake what was troubling him. Will pulled his hands out of his pockets and shrugged. "I kinda miss her. She was easy to talk to, y'know?"

"I told you to forget her. She's not for us." Jake wondered who he'd convince first—Will or himself.

"You're really not going to try to find her, are you?"

Feeling Will's disapproval, Jake came off the couch in one smooth motion. "No," he told Will flatly, the word harsher than he intended—probably because his conscience was bugging him.

"Ah, man, that's crap and you know it!" Will's tone held frustration, disappointment and something very close to disgust. He headed for the front door and then paused. "Y'know? I used to think you were smart," he said, and walked out.

Great, Jake thought, looking at the closed door. The way he was going, no one in the city would be speaking to him.

Adults! Will shook his head in bafflement as he loped down the street. They sure acted strange sometimes. He hoped he had more sense when he got older. Lately he couldn't figure Jake. Mar—Alex was cool. And he knew Jake didn't dislike her nearly as much as he pretended. So why did he keep trying to convince Will to forget her?

Of course, he hadn't been real thrilled to learn she was a cop. Cops were okay, he guessed. After all, Jake was sort of a cop. But Will had seen enough to know that you had to be careful which ones you trusted. And he trusted Alex.

She'd talked to him straight about Cilla. And it had helped. That had kinda surprised him. But he figured a woman just naturally understood these things. At least Alex had seemed to when they'd talked before. And now he needed more advice.

So if Jake wouldn't help him, he'd find someone who would. Will hadn't lived on the streets this long without learning a few tricks about how to get what he wanted. Maybe Nathan could help.

It didn't take Will long to get to the church. He found Nathan in the rectory garden, digging holes in the ground.

"Hey, Nathan," Will greeted him. "What's up?"

Wiping the perspiration from his forehead with the back of his arm, Nathan looked up at Will and grinned. "Nothing much till next spring," he said.

"Huh?"

Nathan stood and gestured at the holes. "I'm planting bulbs. They won't be up until spring."

Will wasn't impressed. He had more important things on his mind. "Oh."

"What can I do for you?"

"I want to find Alex."

Nathan studied him a minute, obviously surprised. "Does Jake know you're here?"

"I'm not a kid. I don't need permission to come to church."

"Sorry," Nathan said, trying not to smile. "I'll rephrase the question. Have you asked Jake about this?"

"He's no help." The teenager scuffed his foot. "He's acting weird."

Even though he hid it well, Nathan could feel Will's apprehension. "Why do you need to find Alex?"

"I'm worried about Cilla," he told Nathan, looking him straight in the eye. "And Alex understands. Can you help me find her?"

Sighing, Nathan thought of the card Alex had left with him. "Maybe." Picking up his tools, he led the way back inside. "Go on home. I'll get in touch with you when I hear from her. Okay?"

Will released a deep breath. "Thanks," he said and left the room. As soon as he'd closed the door, he stopped and waited. He could hear Nathan talking to someone on the phone, and Will wondered how long before he'd leave his office.

He moved quietly down the hallway until he came to an empty room and slipped inside. He figured Nathan had to know how to find Alex. All Will had to do was hang around until he got a chance to take a look at Nathan Garner's files.

Overall it had been one rotten week. Alex eyed with distaste the numerous files spread across the desk in front of her. It was going to take the better part of the day to even put a dent in the paperwork, and her concentration was almost nonexistent.

The tap on the door did nothing to improve her mood. *Now what?* "Come in."

The door opened far enough for Tracy to stick her head in. "Young man out here says he knows you."

Alex sighed and rubbed her tired eyes. "Okay. Send him in."

The door opened wider, and Will stepped into the room. He stopped just inside and stood quietly as if gauging what kind of reception awaited him.

"Will!" Surprise did not describe Alex's reaction. "What in the world are you doing here?"

He shrugged and pushed his hands into his pockets. "I guess I came to see you."

"Well, come on in," she instructed, "and shut the door. Does Jake know you're here?"

"Why's everyone asking me that?" he muttered, doing as she'd requested. "He's not my dad."

Alex pinned him with a level gaze, her look telling him that if he didn't answer she would contact Jake herself.

Will fidgeted and shuffled a bit. "Yeah," he finally said, "he knows."

Something about the way he'd said it made her suspicious, but she let it pass. In the time she'd known Will, she'd never been aware of his lying to her. "Sit down, then," she said, gesturing to the chair on the opposite side of her desk. "How've you been?"

He sprawled into the chair. "Okay, I guess."

She waited a beat. "How did you get here?"

"Took METRO," he said, referring to D.C.'s public transit system.

Alex sighed. It didn't look as if this conversation was going to flow smoothly. She tried a different tack. "How's Cilla?" she asked, and was immediately rewarded by a look of both relief and distress on Will's face.

"Not so good. Someone needs to talk sense to her. She sure won't listen to me."

Alex pushed some the files aside and folded her hands in front of her, wondering how best to handle this. "What's going on?"

"Same thing. Y'know? If she didn't have this problem, I don't think the gang would be so important to her." He sat up straighter in his chair, looking directly at Alex, obviously very intent on what he was saying. "But the way she walks...it embarrasses her. And the guys who recruit for the gang, they'll find a way to make her think they don't care, that they like her, anyway. But it's an act. Y'know? They're clever at fooling people until they get 'em hooked. Then it's too late."

It was the longest speech she could remember Will giving. But she'd learned that though he might be quiet, he cared passionately about some things. Cilla was one of those things. He was a lot like Jake in that respect.

Alex worried that Will was too mature for a kid his age. He possessed insight that few adults in her experience came close to having. "Has Cilla talked to her parents about her foot?"

He lunged out of his chair as if touched by an electrical charge and began prowling the room. He absently fingered several of the books in Alex's small bookcase, looked at a couple of the awards she'd received, studied the framed photos of her family on the wall.

"They don't care," Will finally said. "They say she should learn to live with it."

Alex shook her head in disgust. Why were some parents so insensitive to their children's needs? "What does Jake say?" she asked quietly.

Will glanced at Alex. "I can't talk to him. He's acting...funny. I think he's got some kinda problem."

A frown wrinkled Alex's forehead. "Why do you think he's got a problem?"

He lifted one shoulder, then let it fall. "He's working too hard. He doesn't eat. He doesn't sleep." Will shoved his fingers through his short-cropped dark hair. "And he's doing crazy things."

Alex's stomach took a wild dive. "Crazy?"

Will suddenly looked as if he'd said too much. He shrugged. "I'm worried about him. Jake's cool. He treats me right, y'know? I don't want anything bad to happen to him." He took a deep breath. "That's why I came to see you. I thought maybe you could tell me what to do."

From any teenager, this was a significant admission. From someone as closemouthed as Will, it was even more so. Two speeches within ten minutes. He really was upset.

One thing at a time, Alex cautioned herself. She had some hope of handling Cilla's problem. Jake was another matter entirely.

"Nathan told me Cilla needs an operation. If it can be set up without costing them anything, do you think her parents would give her permission to have the surgery?" She didn't mention to Will that Nathan had said Cilla's parents were opposed to taking money. There was always hope someone might be able to change their minds.

Will brightened. "Maybe," he said. "We'd have to talk them into it."

"Okay, I'll tell you what. I'll see what I can arrange if you can talk her family into accepting it. Deal?"

A grin spread across his adolescent face. "Deal."

"Now tell me what's going on with Jake."

Will sat back down, some of the enthusiasm leaving his eyes, and he frowned. "He's acting goofy. Me? I think it's because he misses you."

Chapter Thirteen

Jake answered the phone on the second ring. "Yeah," he snapped, hoping to discourage whoever was on the other end.

"I see your mood hasn't improved," Nathan commented drolly on the other end of the line. "Would I be taking my life in my hands if I asked you to drop by here for a few minutes?"

Jake ignored the jab but did temper his response. "What's up?"

"I want to show you something I think you'll find interesting."

"On my way." He hung up the phone and headed for the door. Within minutes, Jake strode into Nathan's office.

Nathan held up a slip of paper. "This is addressed to you," he said, handing it to Jake.

He unfolded the note and read.

Jake—

Gone to see Alex. Don't worry. I can take care of myself. Back soon.

                                   Will

Jake released a deep breath. His first concern was for Will's safety. That was closely followed by a small spasm of hurt.

"Seems like everyone in my life is intent on leaving me notes lately," Jake muttered, taking a measure of comfort in the fact that Will's action was one more sign of his growing maturity.

"Maybe because that's the only way they can communicate with you?" Nathan suggested quietly.

Feeling a pinch of conscience, Jake covered it with anger. "How the hell did Will know where to find Alex?"

"Well," Nathan began, looking decidedly uncomfortable, "I had a visitor a few days ago."

Jake didn't have to ask. He knew the answer, but something drove him to confirm it. "Let me guess. Alex?"

Nathan nodded.

"What did she want?" Jake asked, carefully watching Nathan's expression.

Nathan returned his stare. "You know I won't discuss what's told to me in confidence."

Alex had come to see Nathan. Jake let that fact soak in, and the spasm turned into a hollow ache in his gut. He'd played a little game with himself. If Alex had any genuine interest in him, she knew where to find him. That she'd been in this area of town and not bothered to look him up pretty much spelled it out.

Of course, a little voice taunted, he had no one to blame but himself. He'd been the one to order Alex out of his life.

"Will came by to see me earlier today," Nathan continued. "Asked if I'd help him find Alex."

"And you told him where to find her?" Jake asked, not bothering to keep the amazement from his voice.

"Not likely," Nathan answered sardonically. "Apparently Will hung around until I left the office, slipped back in and found her address. And left you the note."

Jake almost smiled. "I'll give him credit for one thing—he's resourceful."

"He has a good teacher."

Jake wondered if Nathan was being sarcastic. "I better go get him, before he finds more trouble than he can handle."

"Jake," Nathan called, as Jake started out the door.

He paused, looking over his shoulder at the man who'd become his friend.

"Before you storm out of here, you might want to give a little thought to what's behind what you're doing."

"Thanks," he said curtly. "I'll keep that in mind." But Jake knew what he was doing. He was fighting to protect his heart.

A harsh rap at her office door saved Alex from having to respond to Will's last comment. Before she had a chance to issue an invitation, the door opened and Jake walked across the threshold. For a split second, she wasn't certain she should trust her eyes.

"Wait for me in the hall," Jake said to Will, holding the door wide.

Will came to a stand, uneasiness making his movements slow. "Hey, Jake, stay cool, man. If you're mad at me, don't take it out on Alex. She's just trying to help. She said she'd help raise money for Cilla's operation."

Catching her breath from the initial shock of seeing Jake, Alex closed her eyes, knowing that was probably the last thing he wanted to hear.

He sent Will a warning look. "You and I will talk later."

"It's okay, Will," Alex said soothingly. "Maybe I'll see you later. Thanks for coming by. And don't worry about what we discussed."

He glanced at Jake, as if appraising his mood, then back to Alex. "Well ... thanks, y'know, for everything."

"You're welcome." She sent the boy a quick smile. "Now go. I'll be fine."

"See ya," he said, and reluctantly left the room.

"Judging by your expression," she commented dryly, "I suppose it would be futile to offer you a seat."

Jake remained standing. "Stay away from Will," he said without preamble.

"Will came to me, Jake," she told him quietly, making certain he didn't see the pain his words caused her. "And although I was delighted to see him, I didn't invite him here." She folded her hands, placing them neatly in front of her on the desk, and waited for the next salvo.

She watched him pace around her office much as Will had. When Jake stopped in front of a photo of

Stephanie, Nick, Jason and herself, she held her breath. It had been taken during one of the family's many excursions on Nick's sailboat.

For several moments, Jake studied the picture. There was nothing in the scene to suggest extravagance. Still, it represented a lifestyle 180 degrees from anything Will and he had experienced.

Because of who Alex was and where she'd come from, Jake couldn't shake the fear that she'd eventually desert Will, just as Debbie had been deserted. At any time Alex could grow bored with this and move on to some other project, leaving Will, and himself, out in the cold. Dammit, he couldn't—he wouldn't—risk a repeat of what had happened to his sister.

After several long moments, he turned to face Alex. "I don't want Will mixed up with you."

She didn't blink. "Do you mind telling me why?"

"He doesn't need to get used to relying on you."

Forcing herself to relax her hands, Alex flattened them against the cool surface of the desk. "If you'd listen to him, maybe he wouldn't feel he had to come to me, or anyone else."

Jake scowled. "What are you talking about?"

Alex wondered if she was about to betray Will's confidence by telling Jake this, but she didn't feel she had a choice. She took a deep breath.

"Will is a crusader. He wants to help Cilla. And, wise or not, he's enough like you that he'll find a way to do it."

"He's nothing like me," Jake told her flatly. "And I want to keep it that way."

"Will could do a lot worse than to emulate you."

"I've been on the streets a long time. I do what's necessary to survive. Don't ever forget that, honey."

"I know you, Jake. No matter how you try to convince me otherwise, you're a good person."

"You don't have a clue what I'm capable of," Jake told her bluntly. It was pathetic how desperately he'd like to believe her faith in him, to encourage it. But she couldn't possibly know what he'd had to do in his life. He didn't want anyone using him as a role model. Certainly not Will. "Will and I don't belong in your civilized world, and you sure as hell don't belong in ours."

She stared at him for several seconds, then shrugged. "Perhaps you're right."

Jake returned her stare, not liking what her easy agreement was doing to his gut. "Did you tell him you'd put up the money for Cilla's surgery?"

"No," Alex told him evenly, surprised at the question. "But even if I had, would it be so wrong?"

"For you? No. For Will? It would be an effective way of encouraging him to count on you." He folded his arms across his chest. "Keep your money, Alex. We don't need it."

Raising an eyebrow, she asked, "No? Do you have a money tree? If you do, maybe sometime you could show it to me."

"I'd say a money tree would be old hat to you."

Alex let out a sigh. "It's not a crime or a sin to have money, Jake. It's how you spend it that matters."

Jake couldn't seem to ruffle her or her cool composure. It made him angry. He thrust his hand into his pocket and withdrew a bill. "Well, here's a dollar. Guess how I want to spend it?"

Apparently his attempted insult fell short of the mark. Alex laughed. She rose regally from her chair and came around the desk, stopping in front of him. "You know something, Lt. Jake McAlister? You're a snob," she said, still smiling. "Worse, you're prejudiced."

It took everything he had to keep his mouth from dropping open. "And just how do you figure that?" Her smile increased, and he wondered if pulling her into his arms and kissing her would put a dent in her composure.

"You don't think you are?" she asked, a smile still lingering on her mouth.

Jake refused to answer, allowing his silence to speak for him. Brushing a finger back and forth over her lips, Alex studied him, deep in thought. He wondered if she had any idea the effect she was having on him.

"Okay," she said after several moments. "Prove it."

"Prove what?"

"That you're not a snob. Or prejudiced."

"How?"

"Come see how I live. I lived in your world and survived," she reminded him. "Think you could do the same in mine?"

This time it was his turn to raise an eyebrow. "But you had help." She laughed again, the sound deep and sultry, and Jake felt the sensitive muscles in the lower region of his belly tighten another notch.

"True. And you have my word that I won't desert you in your hour of need. Fair enough?"

It was a challenge pure and simple, one Jake knew he should ignore. "And how would I do this?" He grinned, a grin that didn't reach his eyes. "Are you suggesting I come live with you?"

It was unsettling just how much the idea appealed to him. It reminded him of those few days they'd lived together in Sondra's house. Before he could stop them, his thoughts began drifting into forbidden areas. Her scent. The taste of her the first time he'd kissed her. The feel of her tucked against him after making love. Memories that were indelibly imprinted on his mind.

"Nothing quite that drastic," she assured him. "I'm having a . . . party next week. At my house. It's formal. Why don't you come?"

Self-preservation urged Jake to tell Alex no and get the hell out of there before she did any more damage to him. But the equitable part of him insisted he find out if she could possibly be right. That was the part that won out.

It gave him an excuse to see Alex again.

Even though he wasn't looking forward to the evening, curiosity forced Jake to show up at Alex's house earlier than he was expected. He wanted enough time to check out the place before the other guests arrived. Seeing someone's home for the first time told him a lot about the person who lived there. And he intended to learn as much as he could about the woman who'd managed to disrupt his life so thoroughly.

He drove down the long winding driveway, stopped in front of the luxurious contemporary house and climbed out of his car. Taking a quick survey of the surroundings, he whistled under his breath. *Impressive.*

A kid who looked younger than Will hurried over to take care of the car. Jake reluctantly relinquished his keys and jogged up the circular steps to a front door that appeared more stained glass than wood. Before he could ring the bell, a dour-faced man, dressed in a butler's suit, opened the door, held it wide and intoned that Ms. Harcourt would be down shortly.

Jake stepped inside. While he waited for Alex, he took the opportunity to look around. The view inside the house rivaled the one outside. He looked down on a great room that defined the term. Several people were busy arranging hundreds of flowers, setting out stacks of dishes and bringing in mountains of food. But even with all the commotion, the place looked stark. It didn't suit Alex. She was fire; this place was ice.

Loping down the short staircase, he covertly adjusted the rented tux jacket more comfortably across the width of his shoulders. He did another quick survey of the room from the ultramodern artwork to the expensive furnishings to the extensive library that ran along an entire wall of the room. He was thumbing through one of the hundreds of books when something made him look up.

Alex stood poised at the top of the staircase, which curved down the opposite wall, watching him with an unwavering gaze. Setting aside the book, he slid his hands into his pockets and sauntered toward her.

"I see you made it," Alex said, as she started down the stairs.

"Looks like it." The dress she was wearing stopped his breath and put his baser instincts on full alert. From the front, the figure-hugging black material covered her from throat to ankle. Except for the slit that ran almost the length of one leg, Jake amended, as he watched it expose a tantalizing amount of thigh with each step she took. He braced himself against the banister and forced himself to wait for her to reach the bottom.

When she stood in front of him, Alex smiled wickedly and did a slow pirouette. "What do you think?"

Despite himself, Jake examined the dress thoroughly. It was outrageously daring, sexy to the point of indecency. The front covered most everything, but the back plunged to just below her waist, leaving her skin deliciously bare. There was no way in hell she could be wearing a bra. Because she'd swept her hair up off her neck, the effect was coolly devastating. And would drive any male with a drop of red blood in his veins out of his mind.

One part of Jake hated the dress, while another lusted to find some secluded corner and strip it off her.

"Back in your working-girl role, I see," he commented lazily, knowing full well that no working girl he knew could afford anything like this. Or look as good in it.

"It's one of my best, don't you agree?" She lifted her hand to his face and briefly caressed his cheek. "It certainly convinced you."

Jake clenched the muscles in his jaw. "Then there's no need to prove it again."

Alex smiled a slow sexy smile. "Isn't this what you expected?"

Frustration warred with anger and another emotion he couldn't define. Before he thought to stop himself, he ran his hand through his hair, ruining the neat style. "Dammit, no, it isn't."

"Yes it is." Alex walked over to one of the tables to inspect the artistically arranged food.

He followed a few paces behind, trying to steady his pounding pulse.

"Be honest. It's easier for you to accept me as something off the streets than from the upper stratum of society." She picked up a tidbit of food and popped it in her mouth. She chewed slowly, savoring the taste before swallowing. "Can you honestly say you feel the same way about me now as you did when you thought I was a hooker?"

"No," he said. And it was the truth. He didn't feel anywhere near what he'd felt then. What he felt now was much more...complicated.

And he hated acknowledging that another part of what she said was accurate. It *had* been easier—and safer—to think of her as a prostitute when they'd made love. There was little expectation of emotional involvement, much less commitment, if she was a hooker. The discovery that Alex wasn't had left him feeling vulnerable. And had triggered his mistrust.

An emotion akin to pain flickered across her features before she masked it. "I rest my case." She picked up another tidbit and offered it to him.

Jake opened his mouth. When she slipped it past his lips, he closed them around her fingertips, holding her captive. Something hot flared in her eyes, before she tugged free. Jake ate whatever she'd given him, but he didn't have a clue how it tasted. The only thing he wanted to taste was her.

He glanced around the room to see if any of the staff was paying attention to them and was relieved to see no one seemed to be. "Who is the real Alexandra Harcourt?" he asked. "Is it possible to know when I've met her?"

"Stick around long enough and maybe you'll figure it out," Alex said gently. Several people were ushered through the front door. She glanced up at them, then back to him. "Now, if you'll excuse me, my guests are arriving."

Jake found the bar and, with drink in hand, stood off to one side and watched Alex operate. He could tell she was deliberately putting on an act. The contrast between the Alex he knew—or thought he knew—and this one was too dramatic. But she greeted every guest by name and listened attentively to what each had to say.

He made a mental note of the guest list. It included a mix of some of the wealthiest people from the Washington political, social and business scenes. Alex definitely mingled with the rich and famous.

When she finally took a break and headed for the bar, Jake joined her there.

Alex accepted a club soda from the bartender. "I need some air," she told Jake. "Let's go out on the terrace."

Jake guided her through the French doors and into the chilly November air. "Interesting group of friends."

Alex wrinkled her nose. "I wouldn't call them friends exactly. Most are merely...acquaintances."

"Then why invite them?"

"Ah," she said, "I have an ulterior motive."

"Sounds ominous." He took a sip of Scotch. "What's the motive?"

Her smile flashed in the dim light. "To separate them from their money."

He didn't want to be intrigued, but he was. "Do you have another profession I don't know about?"

Alex seemed to contemplate her answer. "That would depend on what you consider a profession."

When several other guests strolled outside, Alex sighed, staring toward the door, reluctance clear on her face. "I better get back. My duties await," she said. "Stay and enjoy the night air."

Jake studied her for several heartbeats. "I'd much rather enjoy you."

She turned to look up at him in the dim light and smiled. "I believe that's the nicest thing you've ever said to me."

He took her arm and escorted her back into the crowded room, before he said something else he might regret.

They'd just crossed the threshold when someone hailed Alex. She handed her half-empty glass to a passing waiter and turned to greet the elderly couple heading in their direction. "Senator and Mrs. Sheldon," Alex said, smoothly introducing Jake. "I'm delighted you could join us this evening."

"Now little lady, y'know we'd never miss one of your little get-togethers," the senator boomed. "Specially when it's for one of our favorite charities." He whipped out his checkbook, and his wife dutifully offered her back as a prop for her husband to write on. "That kiddy hospital's been a pet project of Grace's and mine for years, hasn't it, sweetie?" His wife dutifully nodded, and Senator Sheldon handed the very generous check to Alex.

"Thank you, Senator," Alex said, folding the check and slipping it inside the tight sleeve of her dress. "The hospital couldn't survive without your support."

"Well, you just let us know if that's not enough, y'hear?" the senator drawled. "Come along, honey," he said, taking his wife by the arm. "I see somebody over yonder I should talk to." He nodded to Jake and Alex. "See y'all later."

"Enjoy the evening, Senator, Mrs. Sheldon," Alex said, tactfully dismissing them.

Jake leaned close to Alex's ear. "Seems you omitted a few pertinent details regarding your 'little get-together.'"

"Did I?" she said, turning on her thousand-watt smile. "I must have forgotten. Well, I have to leave you now. It's time for my speech." She caressed his cheek again, and he noted her hand was cold. "Don't go 'way."

"I'm not going anywhere," he assured her. Catching hold of her hand, he tried to warm it with his own. Her brilliant green gaze darted to his, then she withdrew her hand and walked away.

The microphone was set up in a corner on the other side of the room. As Alex glided across the expanse of floor, every male head in the room swiveled to inspect her. Jake had an almost uncontrollable urge to smash each one. Damn. He needed to cool off. She'd been teasing and taunting him all evening. She had to know she was slowly driving him out of his mind. And it was having the desired effect. His libido was in overdrive. Hell, he'd been primed long before he arrived.

Halfway across the room, a man reached out and put his hand on Alex's arm. He looked to be in his late thirties, Jake figured, and had an air of success about him. Alex paused, glanced up at the man, then threw her arms around his neck and gave him an energetic hug. Jake scowled. The guy was polished and sophisticated and obviously knew Alex well. Jake couldn't stop himself from speculating whether they'd been lovers. If they weren't, he thought cynically, it wasn't for lack of interest on this guy's part.

The realization that he was jealous was one more problem added to all the others plaguing Jake. He tried to force himself to think objectively. This guy was Alex's type. Glancing around the room, Jake conceded *he* certainly wasn't. What could he possibly offer her that she didn't already have?

After receiving a check from the fawning guy and being waylaid by several other guests, Alex finally made her way to the microphone. Her pitch for donations was delivered with conviction and zeal. But to Jake it was obvious she was playing to the crowd, and the crowd loved it. From their faces, it was clear each one was certain she was speaking just to him or her.

"She's good, isn't she?" said a male voice close behind Jake.

Jake pivoted, ready for a fight. The only thing that saved the man from an instant introduction to his fist was the fact that Jake recognized him from the photo in Alex's office.

He smiled, as if he'd read Jake's mind, and held out a hand. "I'm Nick Saxon, Alex's brother-in-law. You must be McAlister."

Jake nodded and shook his outstretched hand. Nick Saxon's grip was firm, his gaze direct, and Jake knew immediately that he was a man to be reckoned with.

"Sorry my wife and I couldn't be here earlier, but we had a problem with Jason's sitter." He grimaced. "I wanted a chance to speak to you before the onslaught began."

"Oh?" Jake said warily.

"The family owes you more than we can repay for what you did for Alex. And I wanted to personally add my own thanks."

Jake muttered something he hoped sounded appropriate, while sizing up Nick Saxon. The jury was still out on how Jake felt about getting involved with Alex's family.

Nick gestured toward Alex. "She has a talent for putting on a show."

Jake returned his attention to Alex. "Yeah. She's good."

"Perfected it years ago," Nick added conversationally. "For protection."

"Protection?" Jake questioned, still studying Alex's performance.

"Extraordinary beauty like Alex's can be a drawback, even a handicap."

Jake snorted in disbelief. "There're an awful lot of people—male and female—who'd give you an argument on that one." But even as he spoke, Jake recalled her reaction the first time he'd told Alex she was beautiful. She hadn't come right out and said she didn't like her beauty. Still, she'd indicated she wasn't all that enthusiastic about it. Or his mentioning it.

"Remember the saying about not judging a person until you've walked a mile in her shoes."

Jake glanced away from the beautiful woman under discussion and settled his gaze on the man standing beside him. "What's your point, Saxon?"

Nick returned the hard stare unflinchingly. "She'd give it up in a New York minute."

"Her beauty?" Jake cursed softly, his gaze traveling back to Alex. "And you understand why?"

Nick snagged an hors d'oeuvre from the tray of a circulating waiter. "Maybe. You interested?"

Jake pinned him with a challenging look. "I'm listening."

Nick Saxon nodded as if pleased with Jake's answer. "Has she told you about her childhood?"

"Not much," he lied. In fact, she'd told him nothing.

"It was rough—on both Stephanie and Alex. Not that they were deprived of material things. But emotionally?" He grimaced.

"Only thing good about it was it made them close. Alex idolized her older sister. Wanted to be like her. In case you don't know, Steph's a genius," he added casually.

Jake knew. He'd done some digging on his own.

"Anyway, Alex never could get people to take her seriously. Seems some stereotypes die hard."

"Stereotype?" Jake queried.

Nick eyed him. "Beautiful, blond . . . dumb."

Jake frowned and fought down the anger that rose on her behalf. "Yeah, so I've heard."

"Her parents' attitude didn't help, either. They treated her like an expensive piece of art from the time she was a kid. Trotted her out for guests to admire and pretty much ignored her the rest of the time.''

Jake was getting a picture he didn't like. He could see where self-preservation would force Alex to erect a shield to protect herself. ''Why are you telling me this?''

Nick smiled, his eyes unreadable. ''Just giving you a little friendly advice. I hate to see my wife upset, which Stephanie has a tendency to get when her sister is upset. Or hurting.'' Nick Saxon's gaze sought out his wife in the throng of people.

There was a warmth and depth of love reflected in Nick Saxon's eyes when he looked at his wife that was almost too personal for a stranger to witness. The two of them seemed connected, even though separated by the width of a room crowded with people. They sent each other little signals, intimate glances. Jake didn't want to be envious. But he was.

''Anyway,'' Nick continued, ''Alex took this talent she has and put it to good use. Her knack for role-playing makes her perfect for undercover work.''

''Can't give you any argument there,'' Jake said grimly. Her talent had certainly worked on him. But did that mean she was serious about being a police-woman? Or was she simply playing a part?

Nick snagged another canape and popped it into his mouth. He took his time chewing, while Jake impatiently waited for him to continue.

''Trouble is, Alex became a cop to prove she's more than a beautiful face,'' Nick said, once he'd swallowed. ''Now she's moved on to the stage of tempting fate.''

Jake was beginning to see the pattern. Alex felt she had to be more daring than anyone else at what she did. She was trying to prove to the world she was better than the sum of her parts. It didn't answer the question of how serious she was. But it served to double his fear regarding her safety.

Alex finished her fund-raising efforts and headed back across the room toward Jake. Her graceful movements did serious damage to what little remained of his self-control.

"Well, I see you've had a chance to meet and get acquainted," Alex said when she reached them. She gave her brother-in-law a quick peck on the cheek.

"McAlister and I've had a nice...chat," Nick told her. "But if you don't mind, I'll leave you two and go rescue Stephanie." Without waiting for permission, he waded into the crowd.

Alex moved to Jake's side and slid her arm through his. "You seem to be holding your own."

Jake looked down at her, thinking about what Nick had told him. "Yeah. I'm a survivor."

He wondered how much longer this evening would drag on. He wanted everyone gone. He desperately needed to be alone with Alex.

Chapter Fourteen

It was well after midnight when the last guests finally left. Alex closed the stained-glass door behind the last couple and released a sigh of relief. Leaning back against the door, she studied Jake. He looked smashing in a tux, she decided.

"Was the evening as unpleasant as you expected?"

One side of his mouth tilted on a half smile. "I've handled worse. I told you, I'm a survivor."

"Right." She pushed away from the door. "Would you like a cup of coffee, or maybe some tea?"

What he'd really have liked was to carry her to the nearest bedroom and make love to her for the next week. Forget the bedroom—any horizontal surface would do. "Why not? Coffee sounds good," he said instead, surprised that his voice sounded normal.

Alex led the way to the kitchen. It was difficult, but she managed to brew a fresh pot without interfering with the staff who were still clearing away the clutter from the party. She loaded everything on a tray, then looked at Jake. He'd loosened his tie and unbuttoned several of the studs on his shirt. She swallowed. Twice.

"Let's go upstairs and get out of their way," she suggested, indicating the others in the room.

"Lead on." Jake picked up the tray. They climbed the curving staircase to the second floor, then walked silently down the hall to her suite of rooms. Once inside, Alex went to the glass doors that led out onto a small balcony. Her back to Jake, she stood there for several moments, inhaling the crisp air, staring out into the night.

He set the tray on a table and walked up behind her. Running his hands down the length of her arms, he captured her fingers in his. They were cold, and he gently massaged warmth into them.

"Tired?" he asked.

"Exhilarated, actually. We did extremely well on behalf of the hospital tonight."

Even so, Jake was aware that she hadn't particularly relished the evening. "How often do you have these things?"

She shrugged. "Oh, a couple of times a year."

"If you don't enjoy them, why do you have them?"

She glanced over her shoulder at him as if surprised by his perception. "It's for the children's hospital, a cause I support wholeheartedly. The guest list includes people I know who can afford to be generous, given the right incentive. I provide the incentive—a setting where they can be seen doing their good deeds."

But on some level he knew it went further than that, that this was a way she gave of herself for something she felt strongly about. "In other words, they get, they give," Jake said.

"That's one way of looking at it," she said and chuckled. "The fact that their motives might not be the best is irrelevant. Nothing illegal or immoral goes on and their money supports a good cause."

Jake liked the fact that she'd begun to relax. "Did you know I'd hate this dress the first moment I saw you in it?" he whispered against her hair.

She leaned back against him, and he felt her chuckle again. "That bad, huh?"

"Depends on how you define bad. It sure as hell turns me on," he told her gruffly. "Not to mention a good share of the rest of the men present tonight. Is that what you had in mind?"

Alex tensed, then felt Jake's lips move almost soothingly along the nape of her neck. She shuddered at the erotic sensation. She'd chosen her costume with meticulous care. She'd had a good reason. The memories she'd created with Jake the first time they'd made love were infinitely precious to her. But ironically, they included the memory of a man who accepted her for whatever she was—as long as it wasn't who she *really* was.

So tonight she'd decided to play her role to the hilt. But what had started out as an experiment to teach Jake a lesson for jumping to conclusions was about to become her means of protecting her heart. Self-preservation told her that she had to keep Jake from guessing just how deep her feelings ran for him. She didn't think she could bear to witness his disdain or indifference.

Turning to face him, she slipped her arms around his neck. "Then it served its purpose," she said huskily.

Jake speculated whether she was suggesting she wanted to be treated the way she was trying to portray herself. "Was your purpose to drive every man present out of his mind—or just me?"

If Jake had appeared dark and forbidding the first night Alex had laid eyes on him, he was even more so now. He'd cut his hair, and in place of the three-days-plus growth of beard usually present on his hard jaw, there was only a shadow. He looked as polished as any of her cultured acquaintances. But instead of diminishing the aura of danger about him, his formal attire seemed to enhance it.

"Yours is the only response I'm interested in." She smoothed her hand over his chest, testing the hard muscle beneath the crisp, white fabric of his tux shirt. Then she pulled his tie free. "Did I tell you how devastating you look tonight?"

The compliment caught Jake off guard. And irritated him. Her defenses were firmly in place, and she was well into her role of seductress. Just a short while ago, he'd caught a glimpse of the real Alex Harcourt, her inner beauty, her caring, her passion for helping others. She'd opened up to him. And he was greedy for more.

"Thanks," he said. "I can return the compliment. You're so beautiful . . . I can't resist you." He ran his hands over her bare back, fitting her body closer to his, savoring the feel of her satiny skin. "Is that the response you were after?"

A dull ache skittered through her. Only partly, Alex wanted to tell him. What she yearned for was to be accepted for herself, to hear Jake telling her he wanted her for who she was. *Well, you started this,* she told herself firmly, *now you have to finish it.* "It's a start," she said and smiled provocatively.

Jake searched her clear green eyes and tried to convince himself that he didn't care if he was the one she wanted or some imaginary lover. He could make her want him. He didn't doubt that for a minute. For days he'd been driving himself crazy, remembering what it was like making love with her, having her melt into him, around him. All he wanted was to experience her heat one more time. Wasn't it?

He was desperate enough to have her that he'd take her on any terms. Anything that would ease this intolerable ache that had been growing inside him and would probably stay with him for much longer than he cared to imagine.

"If you want to play a role tonight, I can oblige," he told her, his voice edgy. "I want to make love to you."

"Then do it," she said, and drew his mouth down to meet hers.

He groaned and took the kiss deeper the moment his lips covered hers. Without hesitation, Alex matched his passion. He lifted his mouth from hers, watching her through glittering eyes. "I've ached to get you out of this damned dress all evening."

"You should have told me." She nudged off her shoes and stepped back far enough to slide the dress off first one shoulder, then the other. The dress spilled to her waist.

He inhaled sharply. He'd been right—she wasn't wearing a bra. He cupped her breasts, experiencing a primitive pleasure when they fitted his palms perfectly. Bending his head, he nuzzled the soft skin between the two mounds. "What's your price?" he asked, his breath feathering across her skin. "What will it cost me to be with you tonight?" Then his mouth found her nipple and he suckled deeply.

Alex couldn't speak. Her head fell back and she welcomed his intimate touch with a guttural moan.

"Tell me," he insisted. He placed a tiny row of kisses down her torso until he was stopped by the barrier of the dress still bunched at her waist, until he was kneeling in front of her.

"This...is a great..." Her words sounded breathless, slurred. "Ah...down payment."

He looked up at her, his face fierce in the dim light. "But what is the ultimate price?"

Alex's legs suddenly wouldn't support her, and she had to grab his shoulders to keep from falling. "Nothing. Just you..." she whispered hoarsely, "making love to me."

He slowly got to his feet, the intensity of his gaze burning her. "I'm afraid that might be more than I can handle." Alex searched his eyes. This could very well be the last time she made love with Jake, unless she could get him to reveal what he felt for her. She reached for the studs on the front of his shirt and began freeing them. "The bedroom's through there," she said, nodding toward a door a few feet away. "Do you want to find out?"

Her words slammed into Jake, increasing the ache in his groin until it bordered on pain. It was damned difficult, but he restrained himself from sweeping her up and carrying her to the bed. For a reason he didn't want to explore, it was important to him that there be no doubts in either of their minds that she knew what she was doing.

Her dress was still draped around her waist, but she made no effort to cover herself. She looked like a goddess. He held out his hand. Alex placed hers in it and trustingly followed him.

When they reached the bed, renewed urgency just about was Jake's undoing. With Alex's help, he located the zipper of her dress and let it fall unheeded to the floor. All that remained was a scrap of black silky material that served as her panties and the sheerest black stockings he'd ever seen. They stopped at the top of her thighs as if held there by magic. Or witchcraft. The effect was . . . lethal.

He found and removed the pins holding up her hair. On a whisper it fell around her shoulders. "I know you'd rather not hear it, but you're . . . breathtaking."

Alex smiled crookedly. "Do you mind if I return the favor?"

For a split second, Jake looked confused and in that split second, Alex knew that what she felt for Jake McAlister went far beyond lust.

"Favor?"

"May I undress you?"

Jake couldn't remember a time when a woman had undressed him. He nodded and stood absolutely still as Alex pushed his jacket off his shoulders and tossed it aside. She finished removing the studs from his shirt and it followed the jacket. His slacks took a little longer. She had trouble with the zipper but wouldn't let him help.

In moments he stood naked before her.

What would it be like, Jake wondered, to see love written as clearly on her face as the passion she made no effort to hide?

Alex placed her mouth on his bare chest and ran her tongue down the length of it, stopping just short of the pulsing heat of him. She did it with total concentration, as if memorizing his taste and texture. Jake gritted his teeth and fought for control.

Finally she knelt in front of him, cupping him in her hands, caressing the length and weight of him. When she took him into her mouth, it was all Jake could do to keep from falling to his knees.

He'd had all he could take. Groaning as if in pain, he pulled her to her feet and tumbled them both onto the bed.

"I swore I was going to take it slow this time," Jake told her, raw need pushing at him.

Answering need gripped Alex, and she tightened her hold on Jake. His hands raced over her body, stripping off the panties and stockings. When his fingers found the heated center of her, she cried out at the overwhelming pleasure of it.

A guttural sound rumbled deep in Jake's chest. She was so beautiful in her passion. He stroked the slick core of her once…twice…and she came apart in his arms. Then he held her until the tumult abated.

Despite the arousal still pounding through him, the overwhelming feelings he had for this woman, feelings he could no longer deny, softened him and brought out a tender side he'd thought long dead.

When he finally slid into her, one of his last coherent thoughts before the same tumult took him was what would he do when Alex disappeared from his life? Far worse, what would he do if something happened to her?

A short while later, as they waited for their breathing to return to normal, Jake asked, "When are you going to stop playing cops and robbers and find a more appropriate job before you get yourself killed?"

Alex tried to remain relaxed. She'd fought long and hard to be taken seriously. For Jake to still have doubts, even though she grudgingly conceded he might be justified, hurt far more than it should.

"Not until something better comes along," she told him truthfully. "Right now I'm interested in making love with you again."

Jake wanted to argue but found he couldn't concentrate when she worked her magic on him.

Jake awoke just as dawn began painting the sky in fragile shades of pink and purple. He edged out of bed, pulled on his slacks and shirt and gathered the rest of his things. He glanced at the bed where Alex still slept soundly. Momentarily, he considered simply walking out, as she'd done to him weeks earlier.

But he couldn't. Instead, he went to sit on the edge of the mattress beside her. Leaning over, he kissed her bare shoulder. Alex stirred.

"I have to go," he whispered close to her ear.

She turned over, opened her eyes and smiled up at him. "Would you like some coffee?"

Jake chuckled. "We'd probably never get around to drinking it," he said, remembering the pot still sitting in the next room. Her face showed signs of stubble burn. It made her look well loved. He found he liked it.

"That's the idea," she said, and wrapped her arms around his neck.

Alex had brought light and warmth to his usually dark, cold existence. He'd always held himself apart from others, never allowing anyone this close. He savored the foreign sensations. She made him wish for things no other woman ever had. She made him want it all, something he'd never allowed himself to even think about, much less consider.

And he knew it was incredibly foolhardy.

Jake tugged her arms from around his neck. "Later," he said, not quite a promise.

And giving her a quick hard kiss, he was gone.

As he drove away from her estate, the realization went with Jake that Alex had come to mean a helluva lot more to him than was healthy. Damn. How had he let this happen?

At first Jake hadn't been able to shake the belief that Alex was playing at police work. In fact, everything Nick Saxon had told him the night before seemed to reinforce that idea. Jake had already been aware that her motives for entering the force were not the best.

And Saxon had confirmed the fact that Alex took unnecessary chances. Jake's worst fear was that he wouldn't be able to protect her. He knew just how impossible a task that could be. Just as it had been for him to protect Debbie. That was the real reason he'd had Alex pulled off the case. Bottom line was, he'd wanted her out of danger.

The frustration and panic of not being in a position to keep someone he cared for safe came crashing in on him, tying his gut in knots. Someone with an attitude like Alex's would make the job of protecting her doubly tough, if not impossible.

As Jake got closer to home, he was reminded of the sharp contrast between his part of town and Alex's neighborhood.

He wasn't in a position to get serious about anyone, particularly someone as far out of his league as this woman was. Their lifestyles were about as different as they could get. He had nothing to offer Alexandra Harcourt. Nothing.

At any time, something more interesting or challenging could come along and she'd walk out of his life. Or she could simply grow tired of the game and go back to her world.

But a little voice kept prodding him. Was he throwing away the chance of a lifetime? Could he trust Alex? Was it wise?

Or would he be setting himself up for the worst heartache of his life?

Several days later, Alex answered the doorbell to find Stephanie standing on the steps.

"Did you forget your key?" Alex asked, opening the door wide.

"I didn't want to run the risk of interrupting anything," her sister replied, stepping inside.

"What's to interrupt?"

"How did things go at the fund raiser after Nick and I left?"

"Fine," Alex said, leading the way down the steps to the greatroom. "We raked in a truckload of money for the hospital."

"That I expected." When they reached the bottom, Stephanie studied Alex a moment. "I was referring to you and Jake."

Alex folded her arms across her chest and shrugged. "I haven't heard from him."

A look of surprise crossed Stephanie's face. "He must be busy. As I recall, you did say he was in the middle of a case."

"Or he's not interested in seeing me again."

Jake was one of the few men who hadn't either been intimidated by her looks or treated her like some kind of trophy. That alone had put him in a class by himself. And the night of the party had sparked a fragile hope within her that maybe he did understand who she really was. That maybe he did care for her. She couldn't seem to squelch it, no matter how often her practical side told her she was being foolish. But now . . .

"So you're telling me nothing went on between you two that night?"

Alex found her sister's pointed question both unexpected and disconcerting. Stephanie was usually more circumspect, waiting for her to bring up potentially uncomfortable topics. She walked over to the window and looked out, hardly registering the beautiful fall day.

"Yes, something happened," she told her sister candidly, "but I don't think I'm what he wants."

"That's crazy," Stephanie said emphatically. "I saw the way he looked at you. If ever a man was bewitched, it's Jake McAlister."

"That's the problem. I don't want to bewitch him. I want . . ." She let her words trail away. She turned to look at Stephanie. "He doesn't have a clue who I am."

"Ah, I see. You've been playing your usual games."

"What games?" Alex grumbled, but she knew where Stephanie was headed.

Stephanie ignored the question as rhetorical. "Do you love him?" she asked quietly.

Did she love him? Unfortunately the answer was a resounding yes. "Yes," Alex whispered.

"And have you given him the opportunity to get to know the real you?"

Alex started to argue, but it dawned on her that maybe her sister was on to something. How could she expect Jake to know the real Alex if she never gave him the opportunity to see her? If she never let down her guard with him?

If she loved Jake, shouldn't she be willing to take the chance of a lifetime and admit her love?

What was it that Sondra had said? Over the years, Jake had learned that he could trust her. It would never be easy for him to trust anyone. What Alex had to do was find a way to convince Jake that he could trust *her*.

"Thanks, sis." Alex grabbed Stephanie and gave her a hard hug. "I always said you were brilliant."

Stephanie flushed and returned her sister's enthusiastic embrace. "Does this mean you're going to talk to Jake?"

"You can bet on it." Alex picked up the phone. But first she had the little problem of Cilla's surgery to take care of.

Chapter Fifteen

Two days later, Alex sat in Nathan Garner's office while they waited for Will.

"You seem more upbeat than the last time you were here," Nathan commented.

Alex smiled. "Thanks. I am."

"In fact, you look like a woman on a mission." He studied her for several moments. "Would it have anything to do with Jake?"

Her smile grew mysterious. "Maybe."

Nathan grinned. "Now this should be interesting."

Just then there was a strong rap on the door and Will entered. "Hi ya, Alex. Nathan. What's up?" He perched on the edge of a chair, propped his elbows on his knees and waited.

"I have some news for you about Cilla," Alex told Will.

"Cool," Will said, trying, as most teenagers did, to remain nonchalant.

"I've spoken with Dr. Rodriguez from the children's hospital. She's agreed to donate her services to operate on Cilla's foot."

All reserve forgotten, Will was on his feet, letting out a war whoop of delight.

She smiled and waited for him to settle down. "And the hospital is going to waive its charges for the surgery."

Again Will let out a noise that sounded very much like a war cry, then he looked sheepishly at Nathan. "Sorry."

"Go for it," Nathan told him, grinning.

"You mean everything's free?" Will asked.

"Essentially, yes." Alex glanced at Nathan for support. "But you realize that the success of this still depends on Cilla's parents' accepting it. Someone's going to have to convince them."

Nathan grew serious. "Think you can handle it?" he asked Will.

The boy thought about it a minute. "Yeah. I think I can." Then he looked at Nathan. "But you'll help, right?"

"I'll be there to back you up," Nathan assured the boy.

"If they still balk because they consider it taking charity," Alex said, "tell them that Cilla can pay it back by working it off."

Will looked puzzled, and worry began to crease his forehead. "How?"

"Dr. Rodriguez told me she can always use help in the outlying clinic near this neighborhood," Alex told him. "After Cilla recuperates from the surgery, she could work there on weekends and maybe after school.''

''And don't forget,'' Nathan added, winking at Alex, ''there are a number of projects around here that need helping hands. I'm sure we can find one or two that would pay Cilla a small salary.''

The frown disappeared from Will's face. ''We can do it. Can't we, Nathan?''

''I think between the two of us, we have a pretty good chance of persuading them,'' Nathan said. ''Now go give Cilla the good news. Let me know when you two decide we should talk to her parents.''

Will was on his feet again, shooting imaginary hoops in jubilation. ''Thanks, Alex!'' In his excitement he threw his arms around her. Immediately he released her, stepping back a pace, a disconcerted look on his face.

Alex took pity on the kid and changed the subject. ''Do you know where I might find Jake?''

''I haven't seen him today,'' Will said, looking torn between delivering the news to Cilla and doing this favor for Alex. ''But I'll find him for you.''

''No,'' she said firmly, ''go see Cilla.'' She'd made up her mind to talk to Jake. One way or another, she'd find him. ''I'm on my way to visit Sondra. If you happen to run into him,'' she suggested, ''why don't you leave a message for me at her place?''

The boy shrugged, obviously relieved. ''Sure,'' he said, heading for the door. ''I can do that. See ya.''

Once the door closed behind Will, Alex smiled at Nathan. ''Thanks. For locating Will for me, and for the use of your office.''

''You're entirely welcome,'' Nathan said. ''What you did . . .'' He shook his head. ''Well, there's nothing to adequately describe it. And I know it has something to do with all the hard work you do behind the scenes for the hospital."

Alex shrugged away the praise and frowned. "I just hope it works out. From what you've told me about Cilla's parents, they may be the biggest problem."

Nathan winked at her. "You let me and Will handle it. We'll convince 'em."

"Having watched you operate," she said, rising from her chair, "I don't doubt it a minute."

His smile dimmed, and a look of sorrow shadowed his face so briefly that she wasn't certain she'd seen it. "Please," he said quietly. "Don't make the mistake of overestimating me."

Seeing his shuttered expression, she realized that whatever pain he was feeling, he wasn't ready to talk about it just yet. She grasped his hand warmly. Releasing it, she said, "Well, I better go if I hope to have a few minutes to chat with Sondra."

Nathan came around the desk and gave her a quick hug, guiding her to the door. "Don't be a stranger."

Alex looked at him soberly. "I'm working on it."

It was on the short drive to Sondra's that Alex spotted Jake's car parked next to the curb in front of a convenience store. Without thought, she pulled in behind it and cut the ignition. Grabbing her purse, she got out of the Mercedes and started inside.

As soon as she entered the small family-owned business, Alex knew something was wrong. No one seemed to notice the arrival of a new customer. In fact, no one in the place was moving. All eyes were riveted on Jake and a young male, almost as big as himself, he had jammed against a counter. The air was electric with tension.

Alex's professional instincts told her that things were far from under control, that the altercation was about to escalate. Two more teenagers stood off to one side, assessing the situation. She took in their style of dress and the colors tied around their thighs. Gang members.

Gang members usually carried weapons.

Fear pounded through her. Automatically, her hand went to her purse, then stilled. In one sickening instant she remembered she hadn't brought her gun with her. Because she was off duty and planning a visit to Nathan's church, she'd left it in the glove compartment of her car. A moment later, she saw the blue-black barrel of a gun in the hand of one of the young men. It gleamed lethally in the artificial store light.

Out of necessity, Jake's back was toward the two punks. Unprotected. And it made a perfect target! Alex didn't think. On sheer instinct, she launched herself at the teenager holding the gun.

There was a brief scuffle.

The deadly report of a gun.

And Alex felt her body crumpling to the floor.

Then all hell broke loose. The unmistakable sounds of police entering the building. Issuing orders. Running footsteps. Sharp commands to drop weapons. Another scuffle.

Had they arrived in time?

Alex tried to move, to open her eyes, but she was so tired. Must not have gotten enough sleep last night, she thought drowsily. She felt strong arms lift her, gently turn her. She heard a muttered curse.

This time she managed to open her eyes a crack. "Jake," she whispered, surprised at how weak her voice sounded. "You're okay? They didn't hurt you?"

"I'm fine," Jake told her, his words gritty. "You little fool, you could have gotten yourself killed." His tone softened. "Hang in there, sweetheart."

A slight frown creased her forehead. "Don't call me that."

"Sorry." Jake fought back the sting of tears behind his eyes. "Just hang on." He looked around. "Get an ambulance!" he shouted to the gathering crowd.

"It's on the way," one of the cops assured him.

"What the hell are you doing here, anyway?" Fear made Jake's words harsher than he intended.

Consciousness kept fading in and out, and Alex fought to clear her mind. "There's something I wanted to tell...you...but I...can't seem to...think clearly..."

"Save your strength, honey. We can talk later."

"Promise?"

"I promise."

Alex coughed and struggled for breath. "I can't feel anything.... You sure I've been hit?"

Jake looked down at the blood oozing between his fingers. His hand was pressed against the left side of her chest just above her breast. Beneath his palm her heart beat, and with each beat, cold fear pressed in on him like an unrelenting vise.

"Jake?"

"Looks like you might have picked up a scar or two on your perfect body."

One side of her mouth tilted up. "Will that bother you?"

Jake squeezed his eyes shut. "Yeah, something awful." He looked around frantically. "Where the hell's the ambulance?"

"Should be here any minute now," a nearby cop answered.

"Jake?"

"Right here, honey."

"I'm so sleepy."

"Then maybe you better talk to me. I don't want you passing out on me," Jake pleaded, terrified that if she did, she might never wake up.

The shadow of a smile played at her lips. "I think . . . you've said something . . . like that . . . to me at least . . . once before."

"It seems to be a habit with you," he said, his voice husky. "I'm beginning to think you find me boring."

"I guess . . . we're even now," she said, her voice a mere whisper. "I always . . . try to . . . pay my . . . debts."

Jake struggled to keep his face from giving away his fear. "Yeah, honey," he said. "We're even."

Jake fought the panic clawing at him. Their relationship had come full circle; he'd saved her life in the beginning and now her quick action had saved his. He heard the wail of sirens in the distance and prayed hers wouldn't be the greater sacrifice.

She tried to raise her hand to touch his face, but the effort was too much. "Jake . . . I . . ." Her hand fell limply to her side and the darkness closed in.

"There you go, passing out on me again," Jake muttered to her unconscious form just as the paramedics hurried through the door.

* * *

The scream of the siren sounded muffled inside the ambulance. Jake had been adamant about riding with Alex to the hospital. And the paramedics, realizing they were dealing with someone who was not going to be dissuaded, short of a bullet in some vital part of him, finally gave in.

Jake examined Alex's unconscious face, searching for signs that she was still hanging on. He remembered seeing his sister when he'd come to identify her body at the morgue. She'd been so...deathly still, cold, blue. He shuddered as pain ripped through him.

Alex was almost as white as the pillow her head rested on, but he could make out the slight rise and fall of her chest. He glanced up at the swaying IV tube, feeding some clear, anemic fluid into her vein. She needed blood, dammit! Even *he* understood that. But the paramedics had told him that had to wait until they reached the hospital.

"How much longer?" Jake demanded of the paramedic closest to him.

"We're almost there," the guy told him, eyeing Jake as he might a bomb ready to explode. "She's stable. As soon as the doctors get hold of her, she'll be fine."

Jake wanted to smash something. Alex had deliberately taken a bullet meant for him. No one had to tell him that he'd seriously misjudged her. Or had he simply chosen to believe the worst about her as a convenient method to keep himself from admitting how much she'd come to mean to him?

What she'd just done wasn't the act of a cop who wasn't serious about her work. Reckless as hell, maybe. But Alex Harcourt was no superficial social-ite playing at police work.

Because he'd doubted her sincerity, was he some-how responsible for her injury? He remembered what Nick had told him about Alex wanting to be taken seriously. Had Jake forced her off one case for the sake of safety, only to force her into proving herself in a far more deadly manner?

His mind recoiled from the idea. No, he told him-self. She'd simply been in the wrong place at the wrong time. This was nobody's fault. Was it?

When the ambulance reached the hospital, Steph-anie was waiting at the emergency entrance, along with an impressive team of specialists. Apparently, one of the officers on the scene had been able to reach Alex's family. Jake offered a silent prayer of thanks that they had the influence necessary to assemble this amount of medical expertise on such short notice.

He followed the gurney into one of the cubicles and watched while they uncovered the ugly wound in Alex's left shoulder. He couldn't have hurt more if the bullet had passed through him. When the doctor or-dered him out, he flatly refused.

Stephanie put her hand on his shoulder. "It won't do Alex any good if we don't let them do their job," she told Jake gently.

On a rational level, Jake understood that he had to let the doctors help Alex. Help. He'd always consid-ered asking for it a weakness, something that re-quired a person to trust. Something that left a person vulnerable. It took everything in him to allow Steph-anie to lead him away from Alex.

Nick and Jason joined them a short while later in the small private waiting room. The surgery seemed to take forever. Jake paced. Stephanie and Nick sat close together, obviously drawing comfort from each other. Faced with a family crisis, their fierce love sustained them, bound them together. Again Jake felt an aching envy.

Jason, Alex's nephew, sat in a nearby chair occupying himself with a computer game he'd brought with him. He was mature for eight, maybe nine years old and in some ways, he reminded Jake of Will.

Jake paced to the window and looked out, surprised to see that it was only late afternoon. It seemed they'd been cooped up in here for days. Jason came over to stand beside him.

After a few minutes, the boy said, "Aunt Alex was going to take me to get ice cream tonight. We do that a lot." He cocked his head to look up at Jake. "I guess she won't feel much like it for a while, huh?"

He hunkered down beside Jason and had to clear the lump from his throat before speaking. "Give her a few days," he said. "I'll bet she'll be ready for a mountain of it when she gets out of here."

Jason sent him a half smile. "Yeah, I bet she will."

What seemed like an eternity later, the doctor came in to tell them that Alex was going to be all right. "You can each see her for a few minutes," he told the family. "But keep in mind that what she needs now is rest."

Jake's relief was so great that it almost brought him to his knees. And in that moment he silently admitted that he loved Alex more than life itself.

Nick came over and squeezed his shoulder. "She'll be fine."

"No thanks to me," Jake said tersely.

"You can't blame yourself," Stephanie told him. "Alex is . . . Alex."

The fact that no one in the family seemed to blame him for what had happened did something to Jake. "Would it be all right—" Jake hesitated, swallowed. "—if I go in to see her first?"

Stephanie and Nick exchanged glances, then nodded.

"Thank you."

Jake entered Alex's room to find her hooked up to what seemed like dozens of monitors and machines. She looked small and fragile. Not at all like his Alex. He wanted to take hold of her hand, but an IV was inserted into the back of the one nearest him. He had to be satisfied with simply touching her fingers. They were cold, and instinctively he tried to warm them.

He loved this woman. But even though he'd give ten years of his life to spend the rest of it with her, he had nothing to offer her. He'd lived his worst fear today. Not being able to protect Alex. He'd as soon cut off his right arm as expose her to that kind of danger again.

Well, he could do one thing for her. He could get the hell out of her life. What she needed was a man from her world, a man with a similar background, who could talk her into another line of work, something safer.

Something where she couldn't die in the blink of an eye.

The persistent sound of knocking at the front door drew Jake out of the restless sleep he'd finally drifted into during the darkest hours of predawn.

"Yeah," he said impatiently, "I'm coming." He wondered who the hell it could be. Not many people knew about this address, his "real" home—such as it was. He jerked open the door to find the reason for his sleep-deprived nights standing on the other side. Alex.

It had been nearly three weeks since he'd seen her, lying so deathly still in a hospital bed. He allowed his gaze to travel over her hungrily, inspecting for signs of permanent damage. She was thinner, and still a little pale. But all the same, to his eyes she looked wonderful.

"What are you doing here?" he managed to say in a fairly normal voice.

Her thousand-watt smile didn't quite reach her eyes. "You made me a promise. I wanted to see if you intended to keep it."

Jake scowled. "What promise?"

"That we'd talk."

He ran a hand through his already tousled hair. "When did I promise that?"

"I think is was somewhere around the time I got shot."

Jake felt as if he'd been kicked in the gut. He'd have promised her the moon at that moment, while she'd lain bleeding in his arms, if he'd thought it might've helped. He hadn't considered that she'd remember—and hold him to it.

Jake's reception wasn't quite what Alex had anticipated. It was the fact that his eyes seemed to devour her that gave her a glimmer of hope and the courage not to turn tail and run. "I'm here to collect," she said. "Are you going to invite me in?"

Jake's first impulse was to say no. He didn't want her coming into his private space, making memories that he'd never be able to erase. "Shouldn't you still be in the hospital?" he asked, making no move to let her in.

"In case it escaped your notice, it's been three weeks since my little adventure."

He knew exactly how long it had been. To the minute. She continued to stand on his doorstep, looking defiant and fragile. "How did you find this place?"

She raised an eyebrow. "Intuition?"

Jake folded his arms and stared at her.

Alex sighed. "You do remember my brother-in-law Nick Saxon? Government operative? He has access to data bases for tracking down people that are at least as extensive as yours—if not more so," she said wryly. "It took him a while, but he finally uncovered your... hiding place."

Jake should've known she'd figure out a way to find him if she set her mind to it. What he couldn't figure was why she'd gone to the trouble. Didn't she realize she was better off with him out of her life?

"Go back where you belong, Alex. This isn't your world."

"So you keep telling me."

"Why are you here?" he asked again, trying to steel himself against what her presence was doing to him.

"I told you." She raised her chin. "You promised we'd talk."

He took a deep breath, conceding that she wasn't going to give up. "Come in, then."

He held the door wider and Alex walked inside. The front door opened directly into the living room. It was almost bare except for a leather sofa and comfortable-looking chair. "Nice place. Mind if I explore?" Alex didn't wait for his permission but headed toward the doorway leading into the next room.

Jake had no choice but to follow. Not that he minded. It was a relief to see her animated and moving around after the way she'd looked the last time he'd seen her.

"You wanted to talk," he finally prodded as they entered the small kitchen, wondering what she thought of his modest home.

The house was mostly functional. But there were touches of warmth here and there. Just like the man, Alex decided. On one wall of the eating nook was a painting of a rooster and hen sitting on a fence greeting the sunrise together. It added a whimsical touch to the small space. It also suggested that Jake wasn't immune to the benefits of companionship. It gave her a measure of encouragement.

She turned to face him. "Before I was so rudely interrupted by a bullet, I was on my way to tell you that I love you."

For a full thirty seconds, Jake wasn't certain he'd heard her correctly. His first instinct was to wrestle her to the floor and make love to her until she knew just how much he loved her. But that wouldn't change the fact that he had nothing to offer her, that he hadn't even been able to keep her safe.

So he said nothing.

Alex felt the hollow sensation in the pit of her stomach expand. But she was determined to see this thing through to the bitter end. She took a fortifying breath and looked him straight in the eye. "If you can tell me that you don't love me, I'll leave now and you won't see me again."

Jake knew he was trapped. No way in hell could he tell her that lie. "Don't you understand? You don't belong here," he said instead.

"I think we've effectively proven that each of us can survive in the other's world."

"For God's sake, Alex. I almost got you killed!"

"That's where you're wrong, Jake. You had nothing to do with my getting shot. The blame for that lies squarely on the shoulders of the three punks who were carrying guns and breaking the law." She walked out into the hallway.

Again Jake had no choice but to follow.

"You were doing your job," she continued, "I was trying—poorly, I admit—to do what I've been trained to do. Protect law-abiding citizens." She stopped to absently touch a piece of sculpture tucked away in an alcove.

When she finally looked at him, Jake was staring at her hard. "Do you have any idea what it did to me to see you lying there on that floor—" he inhaled sharply "—with your blood spilling into my hands?"

Alex stared back. "It probably came close," she said unevenly, "to what seeing that gun pointed at your back did to me."

Panic began to close in on him. "I have nothing to offer you." He shoved his hands through his hair again. "I can't even offer you safety."

Her heart did a crazy little somersault. It was the first thing he'd said that gave her a fragile flare of confidence. To conceal her euphoria, she walked over to a door across the hall and opened it. She discovered a tiny room, tucked under the eaves. And she instantly knew it would make a perfect nursery.

"Did you know," she asked him conversationally, "that before I joined the police force, I was mugged? It happened in one of the best sections of the D.C. area."

The breath left Jake's lungs. "No," he said, his voice dangerously soft. "I'm not familiar with that particular piece of information. Care to fill me in?" He wanted every detail. Then he was going to find whoever had done it and slowly, painfully kill him.

Alex circled the room, coming to a stop in front of Jake. "Nothing out of the ordinary. We hear it every day. I was leaving a respectable modeling agency in a supposedly 'safe' section of the suburbs. A guy jumped out of a doorway and grabbed me. He wanted my purse. I wasn't too keen on giving it to him."

She took another turn around the room. "Problem was, he was bigger than me. He won. End of story."

It was a fight to contain the blind fury raging through him. "Were you hurt?"

"A few scrapes and bruises. I think I was more scared than anything else."

"Did they catch the bastard?"

"No. And that's one of the reasons I chose to become a cop," she said quietly, again stopping when she reached him. "I wanted to feel as if I had some control over what happened to me."

Jake stood rigidly, absorbing what she was telling him, wondering distantly why Nick Saxon had failed to mention a word about this. Or maybe Saxon had known what he was doing, he thought sardonically. There was little likelihood she'd willingly give up something this important to her.

"But that's beside the point," she continued. "You know as well as I do, there are no truly safe places left in this world."

"Yeah. But some are a helluva lot safer than others."

"Life has no guarantees, Jake," she said softly and left the room.

He suddenly realized Alex was efficiently knocking down each one of his arguments. He took a minute to search for new defenses before following her into the hall.

Alex wasn't certain whether she was winning this debate with Jake or simply holding her own. But he hadn't ordered her to leave. And until he did, she had at least a chance of getting him to admit what she yearned to be true. That he cared for her.

Spotting a door at the far end of the hall, she headed in that direction, hoping it was his bedroom. She couldn't wait to see it. Reaching for the doorknob, she opened it. Ah, she thought, she'd been right. Jake's bedroom.

It was Spartan. A large upholstered chair sat in one corner with a vividly colored afghan thrown over it, as if hurriedly dropped there. The bed had obviously been chosen for comfort. Above it hung the one piece of purely modern art she'd seen so far. It was done in fiery hues of orange, red and purple that swirled together in what reminded her of the emotions Jake aroused in her when they made love. The thought sent a flutter of excitement curling through her.

Jake propped himself against the doorjamb and watched Alex explore his room. Maybe she'd satisfy her curiosity and leave him in peace. He snorted silently. Not that he was ever going to have peace again in this lifetime.

She sat down in his chair. "I like this room," she said. "In fact, I like your whole house."

"Thanks." He shifted restlessly. "Alex, where is this leading?"

She studied him for several heartbeats. "I'm knocking down your arguments," she finally said. "Don't say anything, just listen. We've dispensed with the safety factor—"

"No we haven't." Jake's voice was flat. "I can't live with knowing—" he rubbed the back of his neck "—you're taking risks, putting your life on the line every day."

"Are you asking me to give up police work?" she asked softly.

He wanted to. God, how he wanted to. But he didn't. "I have no right. But even if I did, I couldn't. Not when I know how important it is to you."

Alex saw the stark emotion etched on his face. While she hurt for him, it bolstered her courage another notch. This was the first time she could remember him allowing his feelings to show. "Ah, but you do," she said cryptically. "And it isn't."

He waited a beat. "You want to explain that?"

"You do have a right to ask me to give up police work. I love you. That gives you the right."

"You'd quit?" he asked, incredulous.

Alex nodded. "Being a cop has been an important part of my life for a long time. But there are other things far more important to me now."

Jake suddenly realized he was dangerously close to saying to hell with all his good intentions. He spread his hands, encompassing himself and everything that was a part of his life. "What do I have to offer someone like you?"

Alex restrained the overpowering urge to go to him and show him. She knew that before she could touch him, this had to be resolved between them. "First and foremost, there's you and me, making a family."

Jake felt his gut tighten with a yearning so deep and strong that it seemed to envelop his world. "I don't want a family," he told her flatly. A family meant being vulnerable. He didn't think he could handle that. *But can you handle never having the chance to see Alex pregnant with your child?* a little voice prodded.

"But don't you see, my darling," she said ever so gently, "you already have one. You just refuse to admit it."

"What are you talking about?"

"Sondra. Will. Even Nathan."

Jake swallowed convulsively. "That's not a family. Will's certainly not a typical... son. And sure as hell none of them are anything like your family."

"Perhaps not in the traditional sense. But they grow on you." She stood and began moving around the room, otherwise she would go to him. "I consider them your family. Are you saying you don't want me to be a part of it?"

More than anything in my life, Jake wanted to tell her. He felt his resolve crumbling, and it scared him. "Are *you* saying you're willing to give up everything that's important in your life—for someone like me?"

"No. What I'm saying is that I have other goals now. I want to stay alive, to grow old with you. To have children with you and watch them grow up," she told him softly, pleadingly. "Giving up my job is in *my* best interests."

There was a hole opening inside Jake, a hole big enough to swallow him, but the ache would be with him forever. He couldn't do it, he told himself, remembering the terror of watching her struggle for her life while he sat by helpless. He couldn't risk the pain of losing her. *But aren't you losing her anyway?* a little voice taunted. *Are you hurting any less? You're hurting, she's hurting. How's this any better?*

"The way I see it, we have a couple of choices here. You can reject what I'm offering and be a loner forever. Or you can trust me—trust yourself—and take a chance at happiness." She made herself sit down on his bed and wait.

Could he do it? Could he entrust his happiness—his life—to this woman? Because he knew that once he did, he'd be more vulnerable than he'd ever been.

Jake knew that after today this room would forever remind him of Alex. She had imprinted herself on it just as she'd imprinted herself on him, in him. He read the desperation in her eyes that mirrored his own. Groaning, he crossed the room to her and hauled her into his arms.

The kiss was rough, but she didn't pull back. She answered him with the same hunger. It wasn't until his hand brushed her shoulder that she made a sound that indicated pain. He immediately released her.

"Are you really okay?" His gaze went to her left shoulder. "Hell, I shouldn't even be touching you."

She read the fear and anguish in his eyes. "I'm fine," she assured him. "I promise. You want to see my scar?"

Instantly his hands came up to frame her face. "Don't," he said in a guttural tone. "Don't ever joke about what happened."

"I'm sorry," she told him, "but I am fine. Will you make love to me and let me prove it?"

Jake's answer was another deep groan and a deeper kiss. He stripped her out of her sweater and slacks, while she worked on his shirt and jeans.

When they both stood naked in front of each other, Jake reverently ran his fingers over the ugly scar on her shoulder. "Do you know the first thing I loved about you?"

Alex shook her head, drowning in his exquisite tenderness, in the caring clearly written on his face.

"Your courage." He placed a gentle kiss on the wound. "And your strength." He trailed his hands down to cup her breasts. "And your determination." He covered her mouth with his.

Even through the sensual haze he was weaving around them, Alex didn't misunderstand the significance of what Jake was telling her. He loved her for who she was. She threaded her fingers into his hair and anchored him to her, trying to show him what that—what he—meant to her.

It didn't take them long to reach the melting point. Both were too eager, too desperate to express the feelings raging through them. They were ready as soon as they tumbled to the bed.

Jake slid into her and stopped. When Alex tried to initiate the rhythm that would bring them the ecstasy they both craved, he held her still. Framing her face, he searched her eyes. "I love you."

Alex smiled up at the man who meant more to her than anything else in life. "And I love you."

Then they allowed the erotic oblivion to overtake them together.

Epilogue

Alex came awake with the hazy awareness that Jake was no longer beside her. Glancing around the bedroom, she discovered him standing at the window, staring out into the predawn, one arm propped against the frame. She left their bed and walked over to him. Sliding her arms around his waist, she rested her cheek against the bare skin of his back.

"What's bothering you?"

Turning, he drew her close. "Why do you always imagine a problem?" he asked in his deep early-morning voice that she always found incredibly sexy.

"Maybe because I know my husband too well." During the months since their marriage, Jake had learned to share many of his thoughts and feelings with her. But there were still times when he was reluctant to open up, times when he had to be coaxed. "Is it the Brady case?"

"That's a done deal. The D.A. says he has enough evidence to put Brady and his cohorts away for a long time."

"I should hope so, after all the months of dangerous work you put into collecting that evidence."

She felt as well as heard a chuckle rumble in Jake's chest. "Actually it's your testimony that gives him the strongest case. Without you to corroborate what went on in the alley that night, my account wouldn't be nearly as convincing."

She leaned back so she could look up at her husband in the dim light. "Then what are you doing up so early? We're not scheduled to pick up Cilla from the hospital until after eleven."

Jake's hands came up to cup her face. "She's very fortunate that she had someone like you to arrange her surgery."

She brushed aside the comment. "I'm just thankful that it's over and it was successful."

"Yeah, so's Will." Jake studied her in the pinking light of dawn. "Do you miss police work?" he asked suddenly.

They'd both decided to give up their dangerous work and channel their efforts into working with disadvantaged kids, teaching them how to avoid temptation and stay out of trouble. "No," she told him, returning his searching gaze. "How about you?"

He slowly shook his head, a grin spreading across his face. Picking her up, he headed for the bed. "I have all the excitement I can handle right here."

*   *   *   *   *

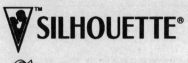

COMING NEXT MONTH

BABY BY CHANCE Elda Minger

Having a family wasn't in Cinnamon Roberts' plans...but a session with a
hypnotist made her totally baby-crazy! Suddenly, gorgeous Chance
Devereux was a daddy-to-be, and hoping that soon he'd be hearing wedding
bells—but could they hope for marital bliss when the hypnosis wore off?

THE HUSBAND Elizabeth August

For five years, Beatrice Gerard remained prisoner to unanswered questions
about her husband's identity and his mysterious death. When she heard
rumours that Joe had only staged his death, she had to risk everything to
find him again...

A FATHER'S GIFT Andrea Edwards

Great Expectations

Jack Merrill was a good catch but, although Cassie Scott was wonderful
with his daughters, she totally ignored his pursuit. She brought life and
laughter wherever she went, and Jack wanted that joy, that smile...that *love*
to be for him!

A BABY FOR REBECCA Trisha Alexander

Three Brides and a Baby

When Rebecca Taylor saved his life, Kyle MacNeill had vowed that he'd
give her anything—but would she dare to make her shocking proposition?
Ask Kyle to give her a baby, no strings attached? It was scandalous—but
she dared...

MANDY MEETS A MILLIONAIRE Tracy Sinclair

Cupid's Little Helpers

Mandy Richardson tried to resist handsome millionaire Connor Winfield
while they were in Tangier together—but nothing had prepared her for his
precocious daughter relentlessly scheming to make proud, penniless
Mandy her new mum!

HAPPY FATHER'S DAY Barbara Faith

That's My Baby!

Handsome lawyer Fernando Ibarra came complete with six adopted kids!
Although Kristen Fielding coped with them brilliantly, she didn't want
even one child of her own. Could he persuade her to become the mother of
a ready made brood...and more?

COMING NEXT MONTH FROM
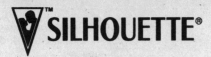
SILHOUETTE®

Intrigue
Danger, deception and desire

RULE BREAKER Cassie Miles
TELL ME NO LIES Patricia Rosemoor
SPENCER'S SHADOW Laura Gordon
TO HAVE VS. TO HOLD M. J. Rodgers

Desire
Provocative, sensual love stories for the woman of today

RANCHER'S BABY Anne Marie Winston
MAN OF ICE Diana Palmer
THE SEX TEST Patty Salier
BABIES BY THE BUSLOAD Raye Morgan
THE GIVING Modean Moon
COWBOY PRIDE Anne McAllister

Sensation
A thrilling mix of passion, adventure and drama

THE LADY AND ALEX PAYTON
Nikki Benjamin
TEMPORARY FAMILY Sally Tyler Hayes
MIDNIGHT CONFESSIONS Karen Leabo
ADDIE AND THE RENEGADE Dallas Schulze

New York Times bestselling author

JAYNE ANN KRENTZ

Full Bloom

Part bodyguard, part troubleshooter, Jacob Stone
had, over the years, pulled Emily out of countless
acts of rebellion against her domineering family.
Now he'd been summoned to rescue her from a
disastrous marriage. Emily didn't want his
protection—she needed his love. But did Jacob
need this new kind of trouble?

"A master of the genre...nobody does it better!"

—Romantic Times

**AVAILABLE IN PAPERBACK
FROM MAY 1997**

JOANN ROSS

Southern Comforts

Welcome to Raintree, Georgia
—steamy capital of sin, scandal and murder

To her fans, Roxanne Scarborough is the queen of good
taste. To her critics she is Queen Bitch. And now
somebody wants her dead. When Chelsea Cassidy,
Roxanne's official biographer, begins to unearth the truth
about Roxanne's life, her investigation takes on a very
personal nature—with potentially fatal consequences.

"JoAnn Ross delivers a sizzling, sensuous romance."

—Romantic Times

**AVAILABLE IN PAPERBACK
FROM MAY 1997**

SUMMER SEARCH

How would you like to win a year's supply of Silhouette® books? Well you can and they're FREE! Simply complete the competition below and send it to us by 30th November 1997. The first five correct entries picked after the closing date will each win a year's subscription to the Silhouette series of their choice. What could be easier?

SPADE

SUNSHINE

✂ PICNIC

BEACHBALL

SWIMMING

SUNBATHING

CLOUDLESS

FUN

TOWEL

SAND

HOLIDAY

W	Q	T	U	H	S	P	A	D	E	M	B
E	Q	R	U	O	T	T	K	I	U	I	E
N	B	G	H	L	H	G	O	D	W	K	A
I	I	O	A	I	N	E	S	W	Q	L	C
H	N	U	N	D	D	F	W	P	E	O	H
S	U	N	B	A	T	H	I	N	G	L	B
N	S	E	A	Y	F	C	M	D	A	R	A
U	B	P	K	A	N	D	M	N	U	T	L
S	E	N	L	I	Y	B	I	A	N	U	L
H	B	U	C	K	E	T	N	S	N	U	E
T	A	E	W	T	O	H	G	H	O	T	F
C	L	O	U	D	L	E	S	S	P	W	N

C7E

Please turn over for details of how to enter ☞

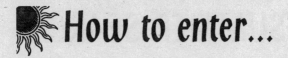# How to enter...

Hidden in the grid are eleven different summer related words. You'll find the list beside the word puzzle overleaf and they can be read backwards, forwards, up, down and diagonally. As you find each word, circle it or put a line through it. When you have found all eleven, don't forget to fill in your name and address in the space provided below and pop this page in an envelope (you don't even need a stamp) and post it today. Hurry competition ends 30th November 1997.

Silhouette Summer Search Competition
FREEPOST, Croydon, Surrey, CR9 3WZ
EIRE readers send competition to PO Box 4546, Dublin 24.

Please tick the series you would like to receive if you are a winner
Sensation™ ❏ Intrigue™ ❏ Desire™ ❏ Special Edition™ ❏

Are you a Reader Service™ Subscriber?   Yes ❏   No ❏

Ms/Mrs/Miss/Mr _____
                                              (BLOCK CAPS PLEASE)

Address _____

_____

_____ Postcode _____

(I am over 18 years of age)

One application per household. Competition open to residents of the UK and Ireland only.
You may be mailed with other offers from other reputable companies as a result of this application. If you would prefer not to receive such offers, please tick box. ❏   C7E

Silhouette® is used under licence by
Harlequin Mills & Boon Limited.